KITCHEN CANARY

J O A N N E   C .   P A R S O N S

ISBN: 0692860452
ISBN 13: 9780692860458

ACKNOWLEDGEMENTS

I gratefully acknowledge the sacrifices made by generations of brave men and women who left their homelands in search of a better life for themselves and their families.

I am grateful as well for the patience and editing skills of Tom Hannon, Jim Berg and Roseanne Curtis.

www.joannecparsons.com
kitchencanary@gmail.com
Amazon reviews gratefully appreciated

Chapter 1

THE JOURNEY BEGINS

GALWAY IRELAND

AUGUST 1868…The rumblings startled her from a moment of sleep. The sun peeked over the horizon. Another night had passed. Katie O'Neil's stomach convulsed as she retched for the fourth time. The puddle of skin and bones sat curled on the wet deck of the ship. She wrapped her numb fingers around the rail for fear of being swept into the rolling sea. A knitted woolen shawl, once a source of warmth, weighed cold and heavy from the ocean spray. She thought, *I'm sure to leave my insides to the fishes.* Rough seas and the cramped, airless steerage compartment robbed life from her each day. The steamship to America rocked and groaned across the Atlantic. She repeated her silent prayer, *Dear God, please lead me to a speedy and painless death.*

One month before, a miracle. A ticket to Boston arrived with an offer to work as a nanny with Cousin Moira. "God answered our prayers, Katie. You're going to America."

"It's not my prayer to go to America, Mam. I won't go." Katie cried and argued every day, finding new reasons to stay. Her protests grew stronger one hot summer day in July. "Mam, I'm not leaving. Nothing you say will change my mind. I'm staying in Ireland."

Teresa O'Neil, patient and wise, nodded toward the door. Once outside, she warned, "You mustn't fuss in front of your father. Come, let's walk along the river and collect mussels for dinner."

At sixteen, Katie stood taller than her mother and shared her green eyes and black hair. The child in the body of a young woman pleaded. "I don't want to go. I'm happy here with you and da. Ireland is my home."

Thin and stooped from years of hard work, Teresa took her daughter's hand. "There's no future in Ireland. We can't survive on the few pence I make selling eggs and the little money from your sister, Eileen. It's your duty to go and send money home."

"America. So far away. I can't imagine it."

"Eileen thought the same when she went off to London last year. Now she writes of the grandness of the city. She sends what she can."

The O'Neils lived a life of poverty in a rural village near Galway Bay. Their one-room mud hut sat on the edge of a farmer's land. In sixteen years, Katie hadn't ventured further than a one-room classroom, two miles toward the Bay.

"Here, put the mussels in my apron. A hot supper will please your father."

Katie gathered a few mussels, "Mam, it will get better here soon."

"There's no hope of a better life. I had dreams as a young woman, too. But, now..." Her voice trailed off as she bent to pick wild garlic, sorrel and rocket, seasoning for the stew.

Katie faced her mother, long legs dangling from a dress fashioned from a bleached flour sack. "Tell me about the great Sunday feasts, music and dancing. I love to hear of the vegetable gardens and family gatherings you had as a child."

At forty-two, Teresa looked older than her years. Her skin was marked and lined from decades of working in the sun. Her memories of the past were Katie's escape. "Please, Mam. I like to imagine myself dancing to the fiddler's gay music."

"No talk of Sunday parties today." The family storyteller, Teresa often shared her childhood memories of happy harvest festivities. She told of times when fathers, sons and brothers farmed the same land. They planted together, and celebrated harvests with family gatherings. An abundant crop brought enough to pay taxes and stock food for the winter. Teresa hadn't shared the stories of herself as a nineteen-year-old wife and mother. Her husband tried to make a life for them on a patch of rented land.

"There are stories you haven't heard. They are not of glorious days. A long time ago when your father and I married we tried to grow potatoes in another place."

Katie walked barefoot along the riverbank, her voice rose, "Tell me. I want to hear it all."

Teresa smiled, remembering, "Oh, we were young and full of dreams. We were cottiers, renting a five-acre plot and living in a tiny cottage not far from here. The English limited the size of the land. It was just enough to grow crops for ourselves. They didn't want us to make money selling extra potatoes and corn. Da was daring and ambitious in those days. He had grand plans to grow enough crops to feed us and sell."

"Did Da grow potatoes in our garden, where we live now?"

"He tried, but the soil is too rocky and dry. He gave up. It was different in our first home. He spent hours tending the fertile earth, rewarded with a healthy crop to sell."

"What happened?"

"Your da was young and proud of the harvest. But, after two years, the potatoes turned to black, putrid smelling mush. He dug them up, and they fell apart in his own hands."

"I'm sad for da."

Teresa walked hand in hand with Katie. "The Irish depended on potato crops. There might be a plate of cabbage here and there, and on holidays, fish. We ate potatoes three times a day. It was a poor life, but we had enough. After two years of the blight, people were starving to death and dying of Famine Fever."

"What did you do?"

"It was a terrible time. Famine devastated Ireland." Teresa stopped walking and turned to her daughter, "That's why you must go." She whispered, "I want you to have a better life."

No longer interested in arguing about America, Katie deposited two handfuls of mussels in the apron. "Tell me more of the story, Mam."

"When the crops failed, your father and I had nothing. We had no money and few things to barter for food. My lungs rattled with the cough. I was too hungry and sick to make milk for our baby."

"My sister, Eileen?"

"No, my love. We had a son, Joseph, born on March 19, the feast day of Saint Joseph. You and Eileen came later."

She jumped in front of her mother, "We have a brother?"

"Please, calm yourself. You're old enough to hear this."

"You kept this secret all these years."

"We did. Those days are too sad to remember."

"Where is Joseph, the baby?"

Teresa looked at her daughter, "Your father tried his best."

"Tried what?"

"It's the worst of my sorrows. Your father never recovered."

Katie's voice rose with impatience, "Tell me."

They walked home. Teresa stopped and faced her daughter. She clutched the apron filled with mussels, "It's more important we talk about you. From the day of your birth, I knew this time would come." She became firm, "You must go to survive."

Katie lingered in the weed-choked garden after her mother went to prepare the mussels. Lifting her head to the open, blue sky, she inhaled salty mist from the Bay.

She followed her mother. The seasoned mussels simmered in the pot over the peat fire. "Mam, please, don't make me go."

Teresa glanced toward her husband, "Hush, child. Eat your stew."

The three ate in silence. Katie's father sat in the only chair in a corner by the hearth. Katie and Teresa stood.

"Mam, dinner is done and da is sleeping. Come outside. I want to hear more."

Weary from the afternoon walk, Teresa struggled to breathe through lungs damaged by the fever. She rested against a large rock. "There was no food. People starved, or died from fever. The English opened workhouses. They were overcrowded and ridden with disease. More Irish died."

"What did you do?"

"We were starving and desperate. I waited with Joseph in our little cottage. Your father set off on a six-mile walk to the soup line run by Catholic Sisters. We hoped broth would help my milk come in. He came over the hill, almost home, to see us standing in front of our burning cottage. The English set fire to all the cottages in the village that day. They evicted us claiming we didn't pay our taxes. They yelled, 'Run, peasants, run.'"

"And Joseph?"

Teresa stared ahead as if talking to herself. "When your father saw the fires, he ran to us. He dropped the soup he carried for six miles. The fires raged. Three hundred ran toward the Bay. There was nowhere to go. We had no home, no food or belongings. I'll never lose the memory from my mind. The English would have liked to see us drown ourselves. Some did, in despair."

Katie gasped and startled Teresa.

Teresa spoke in a gentle voice. "I'm sorry you have to hear this. I want you to understand why you are going to leave Ireland. The English hate Irish, especially Catholics. They tumbled or burned our homes and left us to die."

Katie looked around the great open spaces of the farmer's land. "We have a good life here."

Teresa stood, clothed in rags she wrapped around her body. "It's a meager existence. We live here at the mercy of one man. We will never have more. The English treat us as animals, not humans. I don't want you to suffer a life as I have, under their control."

"How did you survive after the fire?"

"A rancher took mercy on us. His property was safe from destruction because the English wanted his cattle and pigs to ship to England and feed their own. He offered us this, the only home you've ever known."

"And Joseph. What happened to Joseph?"

Teresa pulled her shawl around her shoulders. "I was sick with fever. I had no milk." She looked at her daughter. "He died in my arms, just three months old."

Katie moved toward her mother. "I'm sorry. I didn't know."

Stoic, Teresa stood. "We never wanted you or your sister to learn of this. We've done our best since then. I wish you knew your father as the man I married. The death of our son changed him. He felt the failure, too, when this land didn't grow pratties. After you girls were born, he lost himself in the drink." Teresa looked around, "Our life is not of worldly possessions. It's a simple one, honoring the richness and beauty of nature, and the glory of God."

"Mam, I don't need money. I love wild flowers and songbirds. I can't live without God's good earth and Galway Bay."

"There are oceans and flowers in America. God is there as well. You can't grow old here. We need your help."

Katie asked, "How do we pay the rent now?"

"We have little money. I sew and clean for the rancher. He's a kind man." She held up her gnarled hands. "It won't be long before I can't do it."

Tired from reckoning memories, Teresa walked into the hut with a last word. "America will be good for you."

Still determined, Katie followed. "I won't go."

A gravelly voice rose from the corner of the room. "You will go. You have no choice."

———

The daydreamer who lost herself in stories of Ireland's yesteryears never imagined the journey ahead. Her employer, Charles Brennan, booked passage in the steerage compartment of a steamship out of Liverpool. As customary, the fare was to be deducted from her wages. Katie stood in line wearing the dress Teresa fashioned from a muslin sack, her long, white legs bared. As her turn approached, she moved toward cabins for first class passengers. A voice called out, "Mind ya, now. Stay to your right." The crowd pushed toward an open hatch. She climbed down a rope ladder, lowering herself into the hold. When not packed with emigrants, the steerage compartment held cattle and sheep. Reacting to the stench, she lifted her shawl to her nose.

Old men, women and children poured into the hold. Trunks, baskets and sacks dropped through the hatch. Twelve hundred pressed together in the seven-foot-high, dank space beneath the decks of the ship. Katie uttered a prayer, "Oh, dear God, save me from this."

"Here, lovey. Come." Lost in the darkness, Katie moved toward the voice. "We sleep here. There's five of us. Don't sit up. You'll hit your head." An old woman peered from the horizontal plank. Toothless, with sunken holes instead of cheeks, a black scarf covered her head and wrapped around her chin. Her body blended into the darkness. "C'mon, now. There's room for one more."

Katie looked from floor to ceiling at five wooden boards fixed to the wall only inches apart. The old woman was one of four lying flat on their backs on the lowest one. The woman, looking up, waved her hand. "Right here, lass."

Katie watched others claim their places. Families stayed together. Single men shared. The old woman called out from the section for women traveling alone. Katie hesitated as the crowd pressed closer. With pieces of cowhide tied to her feet, she fought for balance. The hatch closed, taking away light and air. *God help me, I can't breathe.*

The ship lurched ahead to America.

Katie crouched down and curled her body on the edge of the board, her back to the old woman. "Where do I go after sleep?"

"Name's Agnes. Call me Aggie."

"Pleased to meet you, Aggie."

"Ah, there's nowhere to go, luv. Maybe to the deck once a day. Up to the captain."

"How do you know so much?"

"Aye, Aggie listens. I might talk a lot, but I listen, too. The captain has his moods. Some days he orders the hatch open and lets us crowd onto the deck."

Aggie propped herself on an elbow and poked a bony finger into Katie's back. "This is your bed at night and your home during the day. It's where you eat. Hold your sack now. Rest ye head on it," the woman warned, referring to the flour sack Katie carried.

Relenting to exhaustion, Katie laid on her back, shoulder to shoulder with Aggie. She tried to sleep as the ship jousted with the roll of the ocean. Stinking air choked her. Passengers vomited from the rocking of the ship. Rough seas caused waste buckets to spill onto the floor. When sleep came, the roar of steam engines and wails of other passengers jolted her awake. She closed her eyes and drifted off, composing a letter. *Dear Mam, I pray I can return to our beloved home. I know deep in my soul I belong in Ireland.* Tears streamed out the sides of closed eyes as the ship rocked and engines churned.

Katie was one of many passengers sick with diarrhea from the crowded, unsanitary conditions. August storms brought high seas and bouts of vomiting. She spent hours kneeling by the rails on deck, choosing to be windswept by the sea spray than stay in the dark, foul smelling hold. Other passengers, too sick to leave their beds, vomited there.

"You need to eat, girl. There's nothin' to ye. Ye won't survive," Aggie urged.

Katie tried, but her stomach rejected the rations and water. What stayed, ripped through her bowels. If the hatch was closed, she added to the unbearable conditions in the hold.

Most passengers traveled with a trunk or several large sacks of cherished treasures. Katie carried a few articles of clothing, tea and hard tack biscuits. Her old woolen shawl soured from sea spray. *I'll surely die before I see land again. And if I live, I'll never get the dampness from my bones or the putrid smell of this ship from my nose.*

Katie endured fourteen days compressed with hundreds of people in the ship's hold. She wasn't sleeping on a bed of fresh straw. The floor wasn't God's green earth, but covered with vomit and feces. Passenger work crews could not contend with the thick filth of human waste. She clutched her reeking sack and prayed for the rocking to stop. Katie O'Neil daydreamed of her return to Ireland. *I'll see you again, Galway. I'll return to tell you my stories of America.*

When the roar of engines faded, she readied herself. "You won't be goin' anywhere soon, Miss."

She looked at the old lady who laid next to her for two weeks. Aggie knew everything. "First class passengers get off. Then us poor ones."

The passengers stood in the sweltering hold for three hours. The hatch opened, releasing the sick and weary to the punishing heat of the last days of August. Shielding their eyes from the light, men and women struggled to hoist trunks, baskets, sacks, and furniture, and climb the ladder. Katie moved with the swell of humans seeking a life of prosperity. The crowd boarded a tug moving them toward the dock at Castle Garden in Manhattan. When her feet touched the dock, her body continued to sway. One of millions of immigrants to enter the new land, she took her place in line. When her time came, the waif in the ragged dress uttered, 'Katie O'Neil.'

"Medical conditions?"

She startled at the blasts of steam from the ships.

"Medical conditions, Miss?"

"Yes, none."

"Hold out your tongue."

She complied.

"Relatives?"

"A cousin."

"Destination?"

"Boston."

The immigration clerk pointed to his left. She followed his finger to find hundreds of others, some greeted by families, most alone. On wobbly, sea worn legs, she walked into America. No one noticed the tall, green eyed girl.

She approached a carriage with a sign for Boston. The driver winked. "Name's Michael Walsh, Miss. From Kerry. You'll be riding with me."

"I'm Katie O'Neil, from Galway. Pleased to meet you, Michael."

"Let me stow your luggage in the boot."

Katie tightened her grip, "I just have this. I'll keep it if you don't mind."

Michael eyed the sack, and without changing his expression, nodded in agreement.

"Are we leaving now?"

He helped her board, "No, Miss. Several others to join us."

Passengers crowded next to her and across. The hot cabin filled with the odor of unwashed bodies and well-worn clothes. She turned her face to the door. The carriage bumped and bounced. Her bones ached from two weeks of lying in a fetal position and crashing about on a hard board. The horses clipped their way on the two-day journey to Boston. Katie watched the landscape spin by. She thought, *So, this is America.*

Chapter 2
WELCOME TO AMERICA

NEW YORK

AUGUST 1868...Five more passengers, each thin and worn from the journey, crowded the coach. Katie sat knee to knee with a man on the opposite bench. Her shoulder pressed against the woman on her right. Leather curtains sealed out dust and blocked air and light. The man she faced drank from a flask. Other passengers, a mix of men and women, nodded in sleep. The slow, rhythmic pace of the ride made her sleepy as well.

"Irish?" The man with the flask inquired, his voice breaking silence.

Katie replied, "Galway."

He swept his arm around to the other passengers, "Any you?"

"Aye." Each replied.

Swallowing, he swiped the back of his hand across his mouth. "Me, too. It's why I'm riding in a bumpy coach. Takes twice as long, but I won't ride on the Irish graveyard."

They paid attention.

Other passengers stared. Katie asked, "Now, how does one ride a graveyard to Boston?"

The carriage moved at a steady pace. Michael coaxed his horses, "C'mon now. Keep it up. I'll take good care of ye."

The man swigged again, folded his arms on his chest, closed his eyes and snored.

They stopped to refresh the horses. "Michael, what is an Irish graveyard?"

"Aye, it's why I drive the coach. I won't ride over the souls of my countrymen."

Katie asked for more information. "Please, explain."

"The tracks are not a proper graveyard, though dead men rest there. You see, hundreds of hard working Irishmen died building the railway."

"Railway?"

"Yes. Trains run on thousands of miles of tracks carrying people and supplies across America. The Irish did the backbreaking and dangerous work to lay tracks. Took the jobs for money. Was all they could get. Worked day and night, in heat and cold. Didn't get paid half the time. Thousands died on the job or from the fever. They say an Irishman died for every tie laid."

"My goodness. How sad."

"Aye, and for their widows. Nothing for them."

Katie shook her head.

He pointed a finger, "Remember, lass, at least in America we have the choice to work and die. Our only lot in Ireland is to die."

"So, you wanted to leave Ireland?"

"Miss, I'm nineteen years old. Been here near ten years. America is as much my home now as Ireland. I'm grateful for the life."

The passengers rode in silence the rest of the ride. The man with the flask woke when the carriage stopped at 2102 Beacon Street in Boston.

"Katie." Moira called out as Michael assisted her travel weary cousin from the carriage.

Standing on the brick sidewalk, Katie looked up at Moira on the second story stoop of the tall brown building. She dropped her arms to her sides and let her chin fall to her chest. "Come, help me. I thought I'd die before I got here."

The girl standing in front of the brownstone building did not resemble the youthful beauty from Galway. The dirty, disheveled young woman needed a bath and good meal. Moira descended the stairs and coaxed her, "Come, luv, you've had a long journey. I'll help you. It's only sixteen steps."

Katie leaned into her cousin, "I'm too tired to move."

Moira embraced her and quickly stepped back, driven by the odors Katie carried. "Here, now, let's get you cleaned up. A good washing and a cup of tea will do wonders."

"Aye, it will."

Holding Katie at arm's length, Moira commented, "You're so tall. My goodness. And look at the long legs."

Katie's cheeks burned at the reference to her bare legs. She tugged at her dress. "Aye, I see American women cover their legs. And here I'm showing my knees."

"No concern. I'll be fitting you with a long dress. I'm glad to put my eyes on you. How long has it been?"

"We were just children when you last visited Galway."

Moira nodded, "Aye, I remember. I was nine and you were six. I cried when we left."

Their mothers were sisters. Katie inherited black hair and green eyes from her mother. Moira, three years older, resembled her dad, a Murphy. She was five feet, two inches tall, shorter than Katie by four inches, with fair hair and skin.

Moira took Katie's arm and climbed the stairs to the second landing. "I didn't want to come. My father and mother insisted. They think we'll all starve in Ireland."

"It's true. There's no future there. I miss it, too. Our future is here. America is the land of promise."

As they reached the landing, Katie faced her cousin. "And here you are, still with the strawberry blonde curls and rosy cheeks."

"And you, always running about, wanting to race me along the river."

Katie smiled, "I'll be going back. You'll see."

Moira's family survived the famine. Their livestock produced butter, a value to the English. She willingly immigrated to America with plans to marry and prosper.

"Maybe so, but you might change your mind. We can make lives here we will never have in Ireland."

Katie took in her surroundings. "It's so crowded. Houses as far as I can see. They're so tall. I can't even see the sky."

"They are all built in a row. English are mad for the Greek style. Most have four levels. Beacon Street is a wealthy part of Boston. Lots of English who consider themselves the real Americans live here."

"If they're English, why do they have Greek houses? Where are the fields and livestock?"

Moira grinned. "You won't find cows grazing in the gardens on Beacon Street. And we don't keep chickens in the kitchen in winter."

Horse-drawn carriages clicked along the cobblestone streets. Horses pulling cars on tracks carried people in and out of the city. Fishmongers shouted. The iceman and milk vendors called out. Katie put her hands to her ears. "The noise." Pedestrians rushed by. "Why are the people dressed in their finest on a weekday, and in such a hurry?"

"It's Boston, where businessmen and politicians live. They're wealthy English whose families came to America years ago. There are rich Irish as well. Protestants who don't make the claim."

"That they're Irish?"

"Or English, or, Lord help us, Catholic. They are from families who came a hundred years ago. English or Irish, the ones who have been here for generations call themselves Americans. Boston Brahmins. Come in the house, now. Time enough to learn about the people of Boston."

Moira opened the tiger oak hand-carved double doors and motioned Katie into the foyer. "My God." Katie's eyes and mouth opened wide. "So grand. I've never stood under such high ceilings. This room, it's bigger than my home."

Moira nodded in agreement. They gazed at the floor-to-ceiling narrow windows draped in rich blue velvet. "You best take those scraps of hide off your feet. Don't want to track in the dirt."

Katie's eyes roamed a room furnished with Italian and Greek antiques. An eighteenth-century chandelier made of tin and porcelain hung from

14

the ceiling. She reached out to touch the gold-embossed wall coverings, "I know the streets are paved with gold, but the walls?"

"Don't touch. Your hands will make a mark. We're not to touch the furniture except to clean."

Katie stared at the winding staircase. "And where do those lead?"

"To bedrooms. The family's bedrooms. Ours are on the fourth floor."

Katie peered into the living room, "I've never seen the likes. Can we take a step?"

"Just one, with your bare foot. I'll be givin' you a pair of shoes suited for the house."

The two stepped onto an eighteenth century Italian hand painted tapestry. "Moira, there's two pheasants in a meadow painted on the rug."

Moira walked away, talking, "The kitchen is in the back, down one flight. There are stairs to our bedrooms. They are not grand, but clean and warm in winter."

Katie followed Moira to the kitchen. "The cook's in charge. We help in the scullery cleaning the pots."

"I can do that."

"Do not touch food in the larder. The cook gives us the extra." Moira pointed, "There's glass and china in the pantry. We clean that. There's running water. We heat it on the stove."

Katie listened as Moira rambled details. "This kitchen. I might be lost in here."

"The cook sleeps here." She pointed to a blanket folded on the floor in a corner. "Come, follow me to our rooms."

Still wearing her tattered, filthy dress, Katie took in the room. Furnished with a bed and dresser, it had gray walls and a bare floor. Moira instructed, "You have two frocks and aprons, an undergarment, and one pair of shoes and stockings."

Katie moved about, pressing her fingers into the mattress, touching the wooden dresser, opening a drawer. She picked up a chamber pot and examined it. Moira's voice grew loud. "Wear this cap on your head. Always appear clean and tidy."

She paid attention, now. "I'm to have my own room? Me, alone?"

"You are."

"And I'm washing inside?"

"Aye, no rain barrel in the garden here, and we don't wash our hair in the river."

"And this pot?"

Moira sighed, "This house has an indoor toilet for the family. We use the chamber pot and empty it in the flush toilet. Now, wash with this hot water."

Katie lifted off her dress for the first time in two weeks. It reeked of sweat and vomit. Hot, soapy water relieved her body and hair of layers of salt, grime and dirt. Moira ran to the kitchen filling the basin again and again. "Give me that old dress. I'll burn it."

"It took lots of soap and water, but now I can see my own skin."

"Here, I've brought tea."

"Aye, thank you, cousin. Never held such a fine cup."

"Mind you, don't drop it. The help can't touch except to clean it."

Katie glanced at the pile of clothes, "Shoes and stockings?"

"Yes."

"At home I walk barefoot or in winter, tie pieces of burlap or hide 'round my feet."

"You'll learn to walk in them. May have blisters first, then your skin will toughen. The cobblestones, too. You'll get used to them."

Katie dressed, tying up her hair and donning the white cap. She turned to Moira, and with a sweeping bow, asked, "Am I a proper nanny?"

Now impatient, she snapped, "You'll do. Now, finish your tea. We're off to the parlor to meet Mr. Brennan."

Katie dropped her eyes, "Yes, hot tea reminds me of home."

They marched in line to the parlor. Katie did as Moira and stood head high, arms straight, as they awaited Mr. Brennan. They dressed alike. Gray frocks to the floor, white aprons and caps, one tall and thin, the other short and well-nourished. Moira cast her eyes to the painted pheasants. He entered the parlor, "Good day."

Katie daydreamed about this moment. She dared steal a glance. The image of a tall man with a kind face shattered. *Reminds me of a teapot, he does.* She managed a curtsy with a faint, "Good day."

Mr. Brennan wore a dark, heavy suit. His forehead glistened with sweat. He stood just taller than Moira with bits of hair scattered on his oversized, round head. Katie stared at his red face and fat cheeks streaked with purple veins. The meeting lasted seconds. He spoke without raising his eyes. "Miss O'Neil, Miss Murphy will explain your chores and child-care duties. Do not disturb my wife."

Katie's cheeks burned as Mr. Brennan walked away. She turned to Moira. She responded to the look, "We are property to him. Like his antiques. C'mon, then, we have to tend to the little ones."

They found the children playing in their room. Katie introduced herself, "Nice to meet you. My name is Katie."

The children turned to Moira. The eldest, Charles, spoke in a soft English accent, "We don't understand her."

"It's the brogue. They didn't understand me at first."

"I've an accent?"

Moira pinched two fingers together. "A wee one." She lied. "Slow your words. It will come."

Katie recovered and pronouncing each word, said, "All right, children, let's have a tickle." With that, she tickled each child to their delight. They fell asleep as she sang an Irish lullaby.

"Ah, so you can smile," Moira remarked, without returning one.

"Aye, they are such loves. Charles and Margaret are like twins with their dark hair and blue eyes. Virginia, the baby is a golden-haired angel."

"The baby is seven months old, Charles and Margaret, nine, and eight. They miss their mother. They ask for her. So young. They'll forget her soon."

"And Mr. Brennan? Does he pay them any mind?"

Moira shook her head, "Not him. Too busy with his antiques. Just as well the miserable thing stays away. Come, we're going to the kitchen. More to do."

Katie's heart leapt at the aroma of baking bread. "I'm half-starved."

"You won't be eating yet. We've to clean the pots. Don't mind the kitchen. It's always hot. The stove blasts heat all day."

"What about the china and glasses?"

"Leave them to me. He'll take it out of your pay if you break one."

They finished at midnight. The cook laid out leftover ham and cheese with homemade bread. "Katie, this is William. He's the cook."

Katie met eyes with the first black man she ever saw. "Pleased, sir."

The man, towering a head over Katie, spoke in a boy's voice, "Me too, Miss. Call me William."

"Yes, William. I am Katie."

With that, the three ate dinner. Grateful, Katie helped herself, "Ummm, I've never tasted the likes of this."

Moira warned. "Watch for your stomach, it's used to porridge and biscuits. You'll be paying a price if you eat too much."

Moira and Katie climbed the back stairs to their rooms at 1:00 a.m. Always curious, Katie asked, "William. He's American?"

"I don't know the whole story. I think he came here during the Civil War. Ran off from the South and hid until after the War. He's a quiet young man."

A white cotton nightdress lay on the bed. Moira explained, "Mrs. Brennan gives me her old ones. This is for you. Sometimes she passes on other clothes."

"You know her?"

"I help her with a hip bath."

Katie twisted her face.

"I fill a tall vessel with hot water and she bathes in her bedroom. We talk when I bring her tea. She asks for the children. It makes her happy to hear about their days."

Katie put on the nightdress and slipped under the blanket, adjusting to the horsehair mattress. "I've never slept on a bed. I'm used to the fresh hay at home."

Moira knelt, taking her hands. It was the first gesture of tenderness since the welcoming hug. Her eyes turned crystal blue as tears welled. "I know this is hard. I came here on my own because I wanted a better life. It takes courage to stay. You have me. I promise, I'll be here for you."

The long day came to an end. Katie fought back her own tears. "There's been so much to see and learn. I don't know if I can do it."

"You will."

"Thank you."

Moira bid goodnight, "Good sleep. I'll knock at 5:30 to begin our day. Be sure to lock this door."

Katie's eyes closed. She rocked in the rhythm of the ship. Her nose held the stench of the steerage compartment. In the few seconds it took to fall asleep, she thought, *Moira seems older than her nineteen years, and why do they lock their doors in America?*

Chapter 3
MASTER BRENNAN'S LAMENT

BOSTON MASSACHUSETTS

SEPTEMBER, 1868…Another kitchen canary flew into my house today. Now I'm putting up with two useless micks in my own home. The squat red head can't handle the work. Her sniveling and whining make me sick. My wife went behind me to bring on the red head's skinny cousin. Not my preference. Rose insists on hiring these illiterates from Ireland. They come here after sleeping on dirt floors. As if we don't have enough Irish in Boston.

Domestic servants, my arse. All useless, if you ask me. Can't cook. Think a good meal is lumpy porridge. Never seen a bed. Don't know how to prepare one. Their idea of cleaning is sweeping a dirt floor with a twig. Irish, can't tolerate the likes of them. Keep themselves drunk and crying in their brew over their dear homeland and rotten potatoes.

This tall one is fresh from sleeping with the pigs. Stinks of piss and vomit. An embarrassment to the Brennan household.

Harpies are ruining Boston. Thousands still comin', years after the famine. Clans, moving to the north side. Coloreds won't live there anymore. They've gone to Roxbury and the South End. Left behind filthy, falling down tenements for the Irish to take over. There's dozens of them living in rooms together. Even cellars. No water, no heat. Even animals don't shit where they sleep. Rats from the waterfront spreading disease. The fools made it here just to die from typhus and dysentery.

Can't blame the English if they're starving. The Irish wasted their days planting potatoes while the English invented steam power and built factories. We built roads and manufactured clothes and created jobs for our poor. They spun their wheels and wrote sad songs and poems, content to live and die poor. When the potatoes turned black and muddy, they cried and watched the English take back their land. Didn't even fight when we shipped off their grain and livestock to feed our people. Stood on the shores watching ships leave with peas, beans and onions. We took their salmon and oysters to feed our own. They starved to death as we sailed away with their food.

The famine was an act of nature, a purification of an inferior race, I'd say. Irish are and always will be a servant race. An island of stupid, bead counting Catholics. They come to America filthy, sad and poor, and stay that way.

The English are the true Americans. We're opening trade routes around the world and importing silk and textiles. We've built railways, canals and factories. They're good for moving dirt from hills into the river. Hundreds of muckers go out every day, picking and shoveling the peak, making it flat so the English can build more homes. Drink every penny they earn. Worst of all, breed like rabbits. Can't feed themselves or their infants. If they weren't so stupid, they'd take a lesson from us. We're businessmen and bankers, intent on getting rich. They're drunks and fools.

The women are good for nothing. Most daft. Crowding the asylums now, howling and screaming. They're either locked up or walking the streets. I lowered myself once or twice before I discovered Miss Ellie's Parlor. More expensive than the streetwalkers, but a better selection. I much prefer my current arrangement breaking in pure Irish virgins. It's an entitlement for a successful Englishman to have one in his home.

These Irish. A few fought in the Civil War and now they want jobs with the firehouse and police. One or two made their way onto the city council. No mick will see my vote. Only thing worse are the Jews, Italians and Pollocks. Insects, swarming Boston.

If I had my way, all Colored servants in my house. Take William. Here's a man loyal to his master. Been with me nine years, since Charles' birth. Never a bother. He's a man grateful for a job and clean floor to sleep.

William's free now, so I have to pay him. I don't mind. He's a good cook and quiet. Hid here for six years until the War ended. A fourteen-year-old kid, made his way north through the Underground Railroad. His father cooked for a slave trader in Maryland. Got word his son was going to auction so he put him off on an escape route.

The Irish think they've suffered. William was flogged soon as he could walk. He's got the switch marks to prove it. It took courage and backbone, but he did it. He likes to tell the story. His father got instructions to wait for the black moon. He ran William miles through deep woods and swamps toward a light. Left him there, trusting strangers to save his son.

People waited in the woods. Call themselves 'conductors'. Took him north to Wilmington. The kid never saw their faces. He stayed with a white family until they moved him to the next station, Philadelphia. Put him on a schooner headed for Boston. The captain hid him among the free Coloreds on the crew. He ended up at the African Meeting House nearby.

As William tells it, all he owned was the cloth around his waist when he got picked up in the woods. The slave trader kept them near naked and half-starved. The conductors gave him clothes and food. William got word later, the dogs and slave catchers tracked down his father. Beat him to death when he didn't give up his connection.

It took a while, but William taught himself to cook. At first, he made the boiled pork and Indian meal bread his father fed the other slaves. He's come a long way. Reminds me of a young me. That's why I took him in. At fourteen, he fought and scratched to survive. He'll never leave me. There's thousands of freed slaves moving north to Boston looking for work. He's better off here. This job's better than most. He's twenty-three now. Tall, handsome. Black as can be. He thinks I don't know he sneaks off at night.

Visiting his girlfriends, I suspect. When he gets married, I'll make room for the wife. She'll be our first Negro nanny.

My wife, Rose, will fight me on that. Insists on harps. Suppose it's another way to go against me. I'll be watching this new one's long face for months. Another melancholy child who can't cook or clean, like her carrot-top cousin. The one before, the same, so I sent her back.

Stay out of my way, Bridie. It's my wife who wants you here, not me. Tend to the children and keep the house clean. And best make sure my whiskey decanter is full. Leave the cooking to William. I don't want your dirty hands touching my food.

Unlike your father, I work hard for everything I have. I didn't stay poor and pathetic. I scraped and struggled, like a true Englishman. That's capitalism. That's America.

Chapter 4
LIVES COLLIDE

BOSTON MASSACHUSETTS

JANUARY 1869...William poked his head out of the kitchen when he heard the crash. Another piece of Staffordshire china lay in pieces on the floor.

"Oh, God help me. The third since September." Katie dropped to her knees, sniffling, and collecting porcelain pieces of pink roses, and gold and green swirls. "Mr. Brennan will surely kill me if he finds out."

William tended the pork roast. "Won't hear nothin' from me, Miss Katie."

Boston proved difficult. Katie cried every day. Life in a one-room hut in the Irish countryside presented few challenges. Work as a domestic in an American household was far different. She worked ten and twelve-hour days, seven days a week.

Her first hours of the day ended in the parlor. "Look at my hands. They're raw from brushing boots and scrubbing pots and pans in hot water."

"I ache in every one of my bones." Moira spoke for the first time in the day. She knelt on hands and knees, her head buried deep as she swept ashes from the hearth. "And we have floors to scrub before the children wake from their naps."

Katie hadn't adjusted to life in America and in letters to her mother, pleaded to return home.

Mam,
Please, I want to come home. I cannot do the work. I've been here four months and soon will have destroyed all the china.
We rise at 5:30 a.m. and sometimes stay up the night with a sick child. Please, let me save money for passage home.
Your sad daughter, Katie

Teresa depended on the village shopkeeper to read and write her letters.

Dear Daughter
Your da is sick. We need the schillings you and your sister send. There is no work here.
Your Loving Mam

She stood in the parlor, holding out her gray skirt. "I look the fool. I'm not a proper nanny or housekeeper. Can't sew or cook. I swear, I'm coughin' dirt from my lungs from beatin' rugs. My feet are blistered from these hard boots."

Moira removed the last ashes from the hearth. She turned to her cousin, her face streaked in black, "I didn't come to America for the opportunity to be a slave. Stop whining. At least you have me. When I arrived, was just me and William. I was to care for a three-month-old infant and two more children and do the housework."

Katie whined more despite the warning. "Never seen a nappy until I came here, not to speak of velvet drapes and bed linens. Still can't put together a bed the English way."

Moira rocked as she moved a scrub brush back and forth using both hands to clean the hearth floor. She ranted to herself. "Can't eat the rich food. I'm always runnin' to the pot. Mrs. Brennan is no help, stays in her room with the drapes drawn. Never helps with the children."

Katie, always curious, stopped dusting and moved closer to Moira. "Now, why do you suppose Mrs. Brennan spends days in the dark?"

Moira stood, arching backward, hands on her hips. "Reach to the high bookshelves with your cloth, will ya?" Glancing around, she wiped sooty hands on her apron. Collapsing into the cream-colored silk damask seat of a seventy-five-year-old Queen Anne chair, she declared, "I'm tired. No more scrubbing floors today."

"Aye. You need to wash so we can tend to the children."

Moira pointed to the bookshelf, "Don't forget."

Katie stood on her tiptoes and reached the tallest shelf. She swiped a dirty rag across a collection of first edition works of Charles Dickens, "These long arms are good for something."

She drew Moira's attention back to the topic, "Mrs. Brennan?"

"Oh, stays in her dark room day and night. Guess she didn't take to the new baby. Happens to women after birth."

Katie baited Moira, "Her husband's a strange one. Never looks at me. Spends hours in his antique shop downstairs. No use around the house."

Moira's face flashed red as she stood from the chair, "He helped make those babies."

Katie pushed too far. Moira's 'dark days' came without warning. Days she snapped or didn't speak at all, keeping to herself. She did her best housework on those days, beating mattresses and scrubbing floors to a shine. Katie didn't retreat, "Well, I don't think too highly of him as a father or husband. If he's in the house he's hunched over his desk in the library doing business and drinking whiskey. The man is in love with his money." Katie waited for a response. Moira was gone.

———

Charles Brennan owned Beacon Antiques, one of dozens of storefronts on the street level of Beacon Street. It was one of many row houses built on the south slope of Beacon Hill. The home was four stories, including the servants' quarters. Row houses were brick, adorned with window boxes and large brass door knockers. The front doors were decorated with purple glass.

Mr. Brennan worked long hours each day, selling antiques or acquiring items to sell. He conducted the most important business transactions in his private library. Katie served tea and cake. She followed a routine on these occasions. Enter the room, place the tea service on a side table and leave. Mr. Brennan never acknowledged her. This one day she summoned her courage. In her best American accent, she asked, "Is there anything else, Mr. Brennan?" He didn't respond. Blood rushed to her head at the humiliation. She clenched her teeth and marched from the room. She vowed to herself, *Katie O'Neil will not address that man ever again.*

An outing to the market helped Katie forget her disdain for Mr. Brennan. Irish domestics seldom ventured from the home alone. Shopping was the exception. She left a note for the iceman to leave two blocks. The butcher was her first stop. "I've a note from the cook. He wants chickens, fresh-killed, mind ya." She socialized with neighborhood maids and nannies, exchanging news from home and gossip about their employers. Katie bantered with fruit and vegetable vendors. "Good day, to ya'." With a wink, warned, "No bruised apples or sour oranges for me. Won't be paying your high prices today."

After flirtatious negotiations, she often heard, "Miss O'Neil, you drive a hard bargain. Can't resist your smile."

Katie's other outing was Sunday Mass. Mr. Brennan permitted the help to attend church on Sunday, despite his dislike of Catholics. Mass was the one event the girls traded their maids' gray outfits for church clothes. Katie rose early Sunday planning to wear a dress passed on from petite Mrs. Brennan. Once ready, she twirled and danced, showing the back and front of her white linen top and green patterned skirt. "First store bought dress. What do ya think?"

Moira observed Katie in a dress stretched tight across the shoulders, binding at the waist and stopping three inches too soon from her feet. "A bit snug?"

Katie responded to the stinging comment. "It's different for you. I send money home. You keep yours and buy new dresses. I'm just happy for what is given me."

"Not so, Katie. My two dresses came from Mrs. Brennan. My family doesn't need money, but don't have any extra, either. I'm saving for my dowry."

Recovered, Katie continued, "And now," wrapping herself in a gray woolen cloak, "Thanks to Mrs. Brennan, I'll bid good riddance to my old smelly shawl." She stood, shoulders back, head high, chest out, ready for church in her ill-fitting American clothes.

They walked ten blocks together, heads down, fighting January winds. Katie complained, "Moira, we get little time on Sundays, and then back to scrubbing and cleaning. If we lived out, we'd have freedom."

"Aye, but the work is miserable, and the north side where the Irish live is dangerous. Have you seen the ladies in church? They are sickly and stooped."

"I've talked with a few. Most work as stitchers. They spend twelve hours a day in a cold, dark room. They sit bent over a machine or straining their eyes to sew by hand."

"And don't make enough money to send home. That's why you're here. Remember, Katie?"

"Moira, those women live in shanties. Some, outside. Their children beg in the streets."

"Keep to yourself and don't mind them."

"There's twelve people sharing one room. The women cried to me. There's vermin and no toilets. People die from the cough and fever."

"They're beggars. They want your money."

"One poor soul told me she goes without food to feed her children. The husband works on the docks and drinks what he earns."

Moira became impatient. "And you want to move out? I'd be the first to go if there was a better place."

Katie confessed, "I've been sneaking bits of food out of the house. Just cheese and bread to her on Sundays."

"Mr. Brennan will put you out. Do you want to be living on the streets? What we should be sneaking out of the house is ourselves."

"Aye. I'm seventeen, now. Wouldn't mind the company of a lad."

Moira warned, "I'm just turning twenty. You'll be keeping company after I do."

With a final word from Moira, they walked into the church.

———

By spring, Moira trusted Katie with the children on Saturday nights. Her routine, always the same. She crept down the stairs and through the back garden to avoid detection by Mr. Brennan. She stole off to the Saturday church social for an evening of Irish music, singing and dancing. The socials were her chance to meet potential suitors.

"You look lovely. I envy you, out dancing."

Clad in a dress from Mrs. Brennan, Moira primped, "Not going for the dancin', girl. I came to America to meet a husband. Want my own home and children."

Katie winked, "I'm sure you'll catch a good one in your blue dress. Matches your eyes. And your hair."

Moira twisted her head to give Katie a full view of a back chignon and red ringlets covering her ears. "Mrs. Brennan fashioned it." Moira pinched her cheeks pink, "I plan to meet the few good available Irish men in Boston. Maybe one wealthy enough to buy property."

"You want to marry a rich one?"

"Not rich. Ambitious. There's Irish in politics, now. On the police. Been so many fires in the old tenements, the city put on more fireman."

"Where do you hear such news?"

"Listening in on Mr. Brennan talking in the library. Can't stomach the Irish. Calls us useless. Hates the Irish Catholics more. He'd soon see them put on ships back to Ireland. He's mad to see the men getting good jobs."

"Moira, all Irish are Catholics."

"Not so. According to Mr. Brennan, Irish who came a hundred years ago changed to Protestants. They helped the English settle the country.

Back then, Catholics changed to Protestant to fit in. Their sons and grandsons don't claim to be Irish or Catholic, just rich Americans."

"Well, this I didn't know. Now, off with you to find a husband."

Katie knocked on Moira's door on Sunday morning. "C'mon. We have to prepare the children for breakfast. You've slept in."

"Can't wait to tell you what happened last night. I was just in a dream about it."

"C'mon, before he notices." They woke the children and dressed them for breakfast.

Once alone, Moira jumped with glee, "Got my eye on a handsome fireman. Name's Paddy McMahon. I think he's from County Clare." Gesturing around her face and head, "He's got a mop of brown curls and long side whiskers. Just a bit taller than me with twinkling blue eyes."

"Did ya dance with him?"

"Not yet. Haven't caught his eye, but I will."

"For sure."

Six more Saturdays passed without a nod from Paddy. Moira replayed her disappointing evening to Katie on their way to Mass. Walking fast and swinging her arms to keep up with her taller cousin, "Wait, slow down. Let me catch my breath."

"Move along. We'll be late for church. Tell me more."

"He's the center of attention, playing his fiddle and leading the singing." Her pale cheeks turned red, "I'm just too plain and shy for him. He'll never notice me."

Katie, not experienced at giving romance advice, tried. Her arms flailed as she blurted out several ideas. "Well then, next week, faint, and let him come to your rescue. Trip and fall in front of him."

Moira rolled her eyes, "Won't work."

More ideas flowed. "Sit next to him at Mass? Sing the loudest at the social? Give him a wink?"

Moira's blue eyes rolled again before Katie finished the sentence. "Why do I fancy the most handsome lad in Boston? He'll never notice a girl with orange hair and freckles."

As they neared the church, Katie lectured, "Listen, lassie, the fellow will be lucky to have you. I, Katie O'Neil, guarantee Paddy McMahon will be yours forever and you will be blessed with loads of freckled face, curly haired children." Katie grasped Moira's elbow and swept her into the church, passing their usual seats in the back. Scanning the crowd, she stopped at a row and motioned Moira to sit. Paddy McMahon sat to her right. As if on cue, the two turned and gazed into each other's blue eyes. The sparkle in Paddy's eye lit the church.

That day, the three sat together, their lives to be intertwined with joy and sadness for decades to follow.

Chapter 5
THE COURTSHIP

BOSTON MASSACHUSETTS
SUMMER 1869...The glance in the church set Paddy's heart racing for days. He sat in the pastor's parlor and described the meeting. "Father Mark, it was miraculous. I looked to my left and into the face of an angel." Pressing two fingers together, "Just a wee thing, with eyes the color of the sea itself. Strawberry blonde curls peeked from her bonnet."

The priest drew on his pipe, "And how do you intend to pursue this young lady?"

"With respect, Father." Paddy grinned.

"And our work?"

Paddy hesitated. "I'm not planning to mention it. Is that a sin of omission?"

"I don't see it as a sin, son. We do God's work, in secret."

Paddy rose from a stuffed chair to leave. "Say a prayer she remembers me, will ya, Father?"

The priest stood, his black cassock reaching the floor. He placed a hand on his young friend's shoulder. "You are always in my prayers, son."

The memory of the meeting occupied Moira's every thought. She pictured his brown curly locks and the grin that stretched from his left to his right ear. She readied for the social the next Saturday. Mrs. Brennan offered a summer frock for the occasion. Moira fretted to Katie as she dressed.

"How do I look? Is the skirt too long? My hair, what about my hair? Now, what do I say if he speaks to me? Oh God. What if he doesn't?"

"You'll be fine. You've got the gift of gab."

"I've never danced with a lad."

"You've been carryin' on for months. I've done what I can. I can't dance with him for ye."

The church was the spiritual and community center for Boston Irish Catholics. 'Cat Licks', as the English called them, were not welcome in local eating and drinking establishments. Father Mark sponsored socials as an alternative for Catholic single men and women. Moira took her usual spot by the rear door. Single girls sat together chatting and giggling. Paddy played fiddle along with two musicians on guitar and harmonica. The crowd danced to every tune. He chatted with the guests during his breaks, never wandering to the rear of the hall. Moira sat, twisting her fingers, eyes cast to the floor. *First, I wanted him to notice me. Next, I wasn't sure. Now I want him to see me and he doesn't give me a look. Will this night ever end?*

A simple guitar solo signaled the last dance of the evening. Paddy strolled across the hall. Still staring at the floor, she saw his boots. Two feet facing hers. Then the voice, "Are ye dancin', Miss?" She looked up to see his extended hand. The lad with twinkling blue eyes and wide grin walked her to the dance floor. Moira's gift of gab abandoned her. Feet stuck to the floor, hands sweating, she thought, *I'm sure he feels my heart pounding.*

Paddy smiled and led her around the dance floor until the song ended. "May I walk you home, Miss Murphy?"

Moira's temples pulsed. Still speechless, she nodded.

The silent dance and wordless walk home led to more dances and walks. Paddy shared his life's plans and goals. Moira, usually chatty, weighed each word.

She complained to Katie, "I'm mute. Can't find words. If he knows the real me, he won't care for her."

Katie reached for Moira's shoulders, "Show him your true heart."

"I don't know my true heart."

"I'm being punished. Was I wrong for leaving my parents and Ireland because I wanted more?"

"Girl, a lad fancies you. That's no punishment."

Moira started, "It's not that…" and hesitated. "More work to do before the day is over. Let's get on."

As they spent more time together, Paddy asked Moira about herself. "I'm doing all the talking, raving on about the home I'm building. You know I want to break into politics and improve the lot of the Irish. Tell me your dreams."

Moira held one dream in her heart. "I want to raise children in a land where anyone can succeed if they try hard enough."

"An admirable dream, for sure. I'm lookin' for a partner to help me do the same. A pretty one, now, with blue eyes. Can you and I make the world, or at least Boston, a better place?"

Moira put a hand out to him and offered a smile, "Partners it is, then."

The conversation was the first of many. Over months, their gleeful infatuation grew to a deep, mutual love. Moira wrote her family.

> *Dear Mam and Da,*
> *Life in America is harder than I expected. I've worked and sacrificed for a year. I'm grateful to God for sending me a lovely young fellow. He is my happiness. Please pray for me.*
> *Your Daughter,*
> *Moira*

Moira's father replied,

> *My Dearest Daughter,*
> *We are so pleased you've met a young lad. This is a time you need family.*
> *I've learned I have a second cousin in the east of Boston. Please visit cousin Mary Flynn. I have not met her, but she is family and welcomes you. God Bless.*
> *Da*

Moira and Paddy visited Cousin Mary and her husband Declan. Declan worked as a foreman on the docks. They had no children of their own. "Lovely to meet you, Paddy. And Moira, we're just now learning you're in Boston. Please, consider us your family in America."

Declan established Paddy's worthiness, "And how do you make a living, Paddy?"

"I'm a Boston firefighter, sir." Paddy continued to impress, "Building my own home in Cambridge."

"Good to hear, son."

Paddy cleared his throat as Mrs. Flynn served tea. "Mr. and Mrs. Flynn, I'm here to ask permission to court your niece." Moira sat straight up on the settee.

Mary and Declan responded in unison, "Of course."

Declan spoke next, directing his words to Moira. "We expected this and promised your parents you'd have a proper chaperoned courtship."

"Chaperoned?" echoed Moira.

Mary replied. "Yes, dear. You'll be moving in with us. I'm the head seamstress at a dress shop. You have a job there. The owner is an English woman. You'll be a salesgirl."

Thoughts of Paddy faded as Moira sorted the news. She stammered, "Move? Oh, yes. Lovely. A job, as a salesgirl. In a dress shop."

Cousin Mary sat closer to Moira and leaned in. She whispered, "Imagine my shock. Your father wrote his daughter worked in the household of an Englishman. Can't have that. You don't want to be a domestic, dear. It's not respectable."

"I didn't know. It was arranged back in Ireland."

Cousin Mary continued. "I've heard terrible stories of English masters taking what they want from their maids."

Moira's stomach tightened. Her head ached. She stared at Mary.

"Oh, yes, dear. It's a sin. They take whatever they want from the Irish girls, if you know what I mean. Some offer them to their friends as favors. The girls end up pregnant and in the streets."

Moira responded with a mixture of confusion and shock, "Goodness."

Mary placed her hand on Moira's shaking knee, and assured, "You'll be better off with us."

Thoughts ran through Moira's mind as she tried to attend to the conversation. *It's not just me? They take what they want? I thought he was punishing me.*

Paddy was occupied, discussing Boston politics with Declan. Moira thought, *Stop talking, Mary.*

She didn't. "Do you agree, Paddy?"

"To what?"

"Moira belongs with us during the courtship."

"I agree, but it's her decision."

Cousin Mary pressed, "Moira?"

Moira's face burned red. Her eyes stung with tears. "I can't leave Katie."

Mary dismissed Moira's concern, "That's childish, dear. Katie will meet a fellow soon and move along. You can't be worrying about her."

Moira did worry. *What if he does the same to her? I can't warn her. She'd know my secret. God help me. God help her.*

Moira sobbed in Katie's arms the day she left 2102 Beacon Street. Katie offered comfort, "Moira, you have all the reason to be happy. You're to be courted by the most handsome lad in Boston." *Handsome to you, only,* she thought.

Moira smiled and sniffled, "Yes. You're right. It's just, I brought you here. Now I'm leaving."

"We'll see each other every week. You're only a mile on the other side of the park. You can play with the children, and we'll have hours to chat."

Inconsolable, Moira rested her head on Katie's chest, "I love you. I pray God will keep you safe."

Katie hugged back. "Be happy. This is a day for celebration."

Moira worked five days a week in the shop and spent every other moment with Paddy. This happy-go-lucky fiddler proved to be a man of deep faith. His commitment to help his countrymen endeared him to her. "Irish men need to work hard and stop acting like whiskey slugging ignorant drunks." He spoke with the faintest Irish brogue. "You and I will make a difference, Moira."

"Yes, our children will be first generation American teachers, doctors, bankers, or whatever they want."

Paddy inspired Moira to want more for herself, other Irish woman and their future children. They spent hours picnicking on the banks of the Charles River discussing politics. "The Irish left the oppression of Ireland as exiles from their own country. They're here now, suffering rejection and humiliation. We can't let their sacrifices and suffering be in vain. The English don't want to teach our children. We'll open our own schools, provide a good education and instill Catholic beliefs in them."

He spoke of the plight of Irish domestics. Moira agreed, "Irish men fought to free Negro slaves in the South, but their own women are still indentured slaves."

Paddy responded, "And they have no protection from the law, it's a travesty. We need more Irish men in the legislature. I'll fight for that and the rights of women. I've discussed this often with Father Mark."

"He's dear to you, isn't he?"

Paddy didn't tell Moira the nature of their relationship, "Yes, he's been like a father."

"And your own parents, Paddy? You never speak of them. Are they in Ireland?"

The grin dressing Paddy's face faded, "No, not in Ireland. Father's been the greatest influence in my life. We share the same ideals."

Moira reached and touched Paddy's arm. "I'm glad for you."

———

As promised, Katie took the children to the park where Moira joined them each week. "Look at you, so big." Moira smiled as she bounced Virginia on her lap. "Charles, are you learning your letters and numbers? Is Katie a proper teacher?"

The children hugged Moira and ran and played. Katie and Moira gossiped. "Mr. Brennan's hired a Negro woman. Her name's Etta. She's well fit for the job."

"Sleeping in my room?"

Katie broke a piece of bread and shared it. "During the week. He lets her go home on Sundays to her husband and two sons. It's a better life than she had as a slave for forty years."

"And Mrs. Brennan didn't hire a pretty Irish one?"

"He made the decision, not Mrs. Brennan. Etta ran the household on a plantation. Works hard."

Moira quipped, "He figures she won't run off and get married."

"Speaking of married, any news?"

"Not yet, but I dream of the wedding."

Katie clapped, "Me, too."

The two played their game, "You go first."

Moira stood and spun around. "The celebration will be a day long, smashing event."

Katie added every other sentence, "Imagine it, now. Flowers surround the altar. The church organist announces your entrance." She whispers, "The guests gasp at the stunning bride."

"The sight of me brings a tear to Paddy's eye."

Katie pretends to hold a glass. "And then, the party. The church women lay out a feast. The fiddlers play until dawn. We toast the bride and groom, drink, sing and dance into the wee hours."

Moira lifted her arms to the sky, "The wedding guests carry me and Paddy on chairs through the hall."

"And the honeymoon?"

"We'll go to a country cottage on a lake for a few days. I'm eager to be home and start a family and our new life."

"Love's good for you, Moira. You laugh and smile, now."

"Aye, I wish the same for you."

"My day will come."

It was fall. Katie walked home with the children. They skipped along and kicked the piles of fallen brown, gold and red leaves. She made the children laugh when she showed them how she liked to lift her arms and head and breathe in the brisk fall air. She laughed as well at the joy and innocence of the children.

Katie's thoughts turned to Moira and her 'dark days' on Beacon Street. *Moira's changed. No more sad moods. She's living in a lovely home and soon to be engaged. She's happy now. And why not?*

Chapter 6
SHAME IN THE DARKNESS

BOSTON MASSACHUSETTS

FALL 1869 …KATIE forced her eyes open. She struggled to wake from the nightmare. The foul odor lingered. A body weighted her down. *I'm awake. What is happening? Why can't I move?* Her senses signaled her brain. *Putrid breath, a mix of rotten teeth and whiskey, body stench.*

Mind racing, taking stock…*Mr. Brennan…on top of me, clammy skin pressing against my face, stubble scraping my cheeks.* She realized, *nightdress hiked up, hardness between my legs.*

She summoned the strength to sit up. He grasped the sides of the bed and pressed his upper body against hers, pinning her to the mattress. Thrusting his hips, he pushed himself inside. Pain shot…piercing and then bolting from groin to abdomen. Her cries, muted by rhythmic grunts and wheezes from the mouth pressed against her ear. Mr. Brennan jerked his lower body, pushing himself into her, hard, over and over.

The movement stopped. He dropped his full weight. His smell, nauseating. The dark figure exited without a word. She laid still, staring into the darkness. Nightdress askew, bedclothes stained with a lost virginity. *What kind of hell is this?*

After the encounter, Katie lay sleepless at night. She remembered the signs. *The lock on the door. The warnings. Moira knew. Her 'dark days' make sense now. She thought Mr. Brennan hated her. It took months for her to trust Paddy.* It came together. *That's why she prayed for me. She abandoned me,*

40

knowing I'd be next. She cried tears of guilt, not sadness. She deceived me, Paddy, and her cousins. No decent man will marry a used woman. I have no hope of marriage and an escape. I'm dirty now, used.

Ashamed, Katie withdrew into herself. Etta noticed, "What's wrong, Miss Katie? You walkin' 'round with a long face. Ain't hummin' Irish songs. Can't even see them pretty eyes. You always looking to the floor."

"I'm not well, Etta. Please, bring tea to the library? I have to see to the children."

"'Course. I been watchin', Etta knows. You afraid of Mr. Brennan. I see. Let me take the tea."

Katie moved her small dresser against the door. The next night the dresser was gone, pieces of clothing left scattered on the floor. She laid in bed coiled in a ball, hoping to protect herself from his assaults. There was no escaping. If she slept, she'd wake, sensing him. He rolled her onto her back. Without speaking, he lifted her nightdress to probe her breasts and private parts. Sounds of his pleasure intruded the silence. She stiffened her body, arms to her sides and fought nausea. When he was hard, he mounted, jerked and pushed until he satisfied himself. Katie turned her face to the wall to transcend herself during the assaults. *I can count twenty shades of green on the hills of Galway. Oh, I'm walking barefoot along the river. It's so peaceful. Mam and da are at the door, welcoming me home.*

Moira, comfortably settled with cousins Mary and Declan, waited for Katie before Sunday Mass. Katie approached, gaunt and expressionless. There was no bounce in her step, no smile or wave of recognition. She did not skip and walk, swishing her green tweed skirt. Moira recognized the darkness behind Katie's eyes. She saw the sense of hopelessness. "Here, let me hug you."

Katie stiffened at the touch and stared ahead. She walked alone into church. Thoughts swirled in her mind. *I'm angry, Moira. You abandoned me. I slave all day and spend my nights in fear. You brought me to America and led me into a trap.*

41

She rushed home, avoiding contact with others. Instead, she spent time alone planning a way out. Her sense of hopelessness deepened. A domestic position had advantages. No job in Boston paid the same or provided food and housing. Irish tenements and rooming houses were disease ridden and dangerous for women. British soldiers and sailors roamed the waterfront on the north side of Boston where the Irish lived. They came for the prostitutes and liquor. The streets, dangerous dark, narrow winding alleys.

Returning to Ireland was not a choice. Life there was dire. Her father, now descended into despair, and numbed with his home brewed whiskey. Her mother's last letter was desperate.

My hands are crippled. I can't clean or sew for rent. Your sister is married with a child and cannot help. We barely survive with the schillings you send.

Katie prepared for confession before Christmas. She knelt on one side of the curtain, knowing Father Mark sat on the other. "Good Morning. Please begin."

"Forgive me, Father. I committed sins against chastity."

Father Mark kept many secrets. He spoke softly, "God is good. He forgives us as long as we have true contrition."

"Yes. I am truly sorry."

He offered understanding and compassion. "Pray to the Lord for forgiveness. Express your sorrow and resolve to stay chaste."

Katie looked at the curtain, "Father, I can pray for forgiveness and I am sorry, but I cannot promise the Lord I'll be chaste."

At that, Katie left the church. The priest followed. "Katie, please. Let me help."

"No, Father. I'll pray and prepare my soul for Christmas."

He shivered, standing in the cold churchyard, "I'm worried. You're troubled. Please, talk to me."

"It's too hard to talk about. Thank you, Father. I must run off."

———

Winter passed. Katie lived in isolation. Shame stole her appetite for food and taste for the company of others. Thoughts of confronting Moira occupied her mind. She didn't share her secret with the household help, but learned they, too, suffered at the hands of others. She and Etta chatted as they washed the pots. "How are your boys?"

"Miss Katie, those two rascals keep me busy. Their daddy walks them to the black school each day or they're sure to run off."

Katie wondered, "Do you wish you lived home?"

"I do, honey, but we need money. Me and my husband moved from the South expecting a free life, with paying jobs. Not so. White people don't want to hire my Nathan, 'cept to clean up after them. Half the time they don't give him his pay. Nathan's a blacksmith, a smart man."

"Same for me, Etta. I'd be living in the tenements on the north side working for pennies if I left here."

"Ain't no place for you, Miss Katie. Free Negroes lived there during the war. It's where the Underground Railroad hid runaway slaves. Got so crowded, when the War ended the blacks moved on. There's nothin' but wooden shacks and shanties. It's a dangerous place, street walkers, drunks, sailors…"

"Irish live there, I hear."

"They do. Crammed together. Dozens living in one room and no running water. No place for a young woman or children. There's rats making people sick."

She changed the subject, "How old are your boys, Etta."

"They're twins. Born nine years ago, before we got freed."

Katie talked more than she washed. "It must have been hard being a slave. At least your family was together."

"I didn't see much of Nathan. I ran the big house for the missus. Slept there. Nathan stayed in the men's slave quarters. Sneaked around once in a while. Took a beatin' if we got caught."

"And the children. Did they stay in the big house?"

Etta stopped scrubbing a big pot. "Child, we was slaves. Didn't have no family life. Other women slaves raised my boys to be slaves. If we weren't freed, they'd been sold."

Katie blushed, "Sorry, Etta. I had no idea. I'm glad the family is together now. I'm sure they're lovely children."

"Oh, they that, all right. They half white. Me and Nathan love 'em, but Negroes don't. Whites don't, neither. You ain't one of them if you got one drop of Negro blood. Their real daddy is the master, Mr. Welton."

"Oh, Etta. I didn't know."

"A course you didn't. Not your doin'. Slaves didn't have no life of their own. We belonged to the master. Least my boys look black. There was some who looked white as you."

"I don't understand."

"Lot of the masters, they liked the light colored black women. Mr. Welton, he was different. He liked his women dark."

"Etta, were there white slaves?"

"Sure were. When the masters was with the light skinned blacks, those babies came out white. Not a trace of black on them. Still, they was slaves."

"What happened to them?"

"Nothin'. They was just slaves. Saw some auctioned. Little girls with white skin, blue eyes and straight brown hair. The white masters liked them. Took them as mistresses. Young girls, fourteen, fifteen."

Katie repeated Etta's words, "The white masters and the young white girls?"

"Yup. They free now. Trying to pass. Trouble is, they talk like black slaves. Manners give them away. There'll be plenty of trouble when they start having black babies with their white husbands."

"Etta, what a terrible lot for them."

"Some think it's why Northerners was so upset about slavery. Not for us blacks, for the whites."

Katie repeated Etta's words again, "White masters and young white girls."

Etta reached to touch Katie's arm, "There's one thing you and me know, Miss Katie. Masters take what they want. Don't they? South or North."

————

Moira watched for Katie at church each Sunday. She attempted lighthearted chatter. Katie walked passed, attending Mass alone. She left as soon as it ended. She did not want to listen to stories of Moira's courtship. "I'll be off now, back to the children."

"Can I walk with you, please? Wait for me."

Each week Katie brushed past without responding. *No, Moira, you can't walk with me. You sacrificed me for your own happiness.*

Katie's loss of appetite did not go unnoticed. "Miss Katie, I cooked turkey soup. Lots of carrots and onions."

"William, I thank you. Just not hungry right now."

"Miss Katie, I know 'bout hunger. You lookin' real bony. You need to eat. Can't be starvin'."

Again, Katie moved the attention from herself, "Did you go hungry?"

"Yes, ma'am. My daddy did the cookin', but he got a switchin' if he stole extra food. The master kept us lean and close to naked. Too weak to run. When you got sold, the new master fattened you up."

"I'm happy you escaped, William."

"Yes, ma'am. I'm lucky. Mr. Brennan took me in. The rest of the whites don't want the freed slaves. The Negroes ain't welcome, North or South. Thousands of freed slaves got no jobs, no place to live. At least on the plantation, there's food and a place to sleep. They worse off free. This is a good job. Mr. Brennan don't beat me and lets me sleep inside. Wish my daddy could see how fine I'm doing."

"I'm sure he's looking at you from heaven and smiling."

"Eat up, Miss Katie."

———

Katie's spirits were not renewed with the onset of spring. She didn't lift her face to the warm sun. Buds burst from the trees without notice. Her world remained gray and clouded. There was no sleep, as she waited for him to appear to take in her young body and run his sweaty hands over her breasts. When he drank too much whiskey, he forced himself into her mouth with demands she make him hard. And if she did not arouse him, he ran his rough hands up and down her body to pleasure himself.

In rare moments during the day, the sweet voices of the children distracted Katie enough to smile and laugh. The youngest was two and Charles and Margaret, ten and nine. Katie filled her days teaching and playing with them. Her English improved as she reviewed the letters of the alphabet and read primers. They were the joy in her life.

At times, she retreated to daydreams, allowing herself to imagine being a mother. *I'll be a doting mam to my own children. We'll say our prayers and I'll sing them to sleep each night.* She dared to add a husband and home to her fantasies. *Their da will be fetchingly handsome and kind. We'll live in a cottage near Galway Bay with lilac trees, and grow vegetables in the garden.*

Katie escaped her real world with thoughts of another life. They brought comfort, and for the moment tempered the rage burning inside.

Chapter 7
RECONCILIATION

BOSTON MASSACHUSETTS

SPRING 1870...The earth thawed and the warm sun beckoned bare trees to release buds. Bostonians, eager for spring, emerged after the darkness of winter. Streets burst with activity. Market vendors offered fresh vegetables from warmer states and shop windows displayed spring fashions. Life returned to Boston.

Paddy drove the last nail into the house. He took a moment to reflect. *My children will grow up here.* He walked Moira through the home. "It's called Gothic Revival."

Moira was quiet, observing Paddy's work. "It's lovely."

"The roof is pitched to help the snow fall off. I extended the windows into the gables for effect. Do you like it?"

"Yes, of course."

"The porch is the width of the house." He put his arm around her shoulders and looked at her. "I can imagine sitting there on a summer evening."

"You can be proud of yourself, Paddy."

"I am. It's taken every minute and penny I've had for the last year. Let's go inside."

They entered the central room. "It's post and beam. I've located the hearth in the center so the heat will disburse all around. Moira, do you like it? You're not saying much."

"Yes, for sure. I'm amazed that you did this."

"I'm amazed with you. There will come a day when you'll share this with me."

Moira and Paddy held hands and walked about the garden. Paddy's satisfaction with himself showed. "We'll plant flowers and vegetables here where the sun shines all day. Oh, it will be a wonderful life for you, me and our children."

Eager to welcome a wife into his life, he summoned his courage and approached the Flynns. Dressed in his Sunday waistcoat and white shirt, Paddy delivered his rehearsed speech. "Mr. and Mrs. Flynn, I am grateful for your kindness toward Moira and for your hospitality. Moira and I met one year ago. I loved her at first sight. She tried my patience, making me wait for her to return my love. We share the same faith in God and dream of raising a family. I will stay by her side for the rest of our lives."

"Paddy, we are so pleased. We've seen the love grow between you."

"Mr. and Mrs. Flynn, may I have your permission to marry Moira and care for her and our future children?"

Mrs. Flynn rushed to hug a blushing Paddy. Mr. Flynn extended his hand. "You have our blessings. Please, call us Declan and Mary. We're family."

Paddy smiled his wide grin and shook Declan's hand.

"When will you propose?"

Reacting to the positive response, Paddy stood erect, his voice growing louder, "Easter Sunday. I'm planning a walk along the Charles after Mass."

Mary clapped, "We'll celebrate with a ham dinner. It will be a joyous Easter and start of spring."

———

There was no joy for the approach of Easter and spring days for Katie. As Sunday Mass finished, she rushed from church, not noticing the crocuses and tulips. Father Mark followed her to the street. "Child, we haven't chatted this winter. I'm concerned."

"The little ones have colds. I'm busy caring for them."

He looked at the thin, dark-eyed young woman, "Let me help."

Katie dismissed his concerns and walked away, "Good day, Father."

Father Mark found Moira lighting a candle in the church. "Moira, please. Talk to me. Katie is distraught and refuses my help. I've watched you suffer this winter as well. You've grown distant from each other."

Moira knelt, hands folded in prayer, as the priest went on. "I'm worried about you both." He extended his hand.

Moira stood and took his hand. "I'm tired from carrying the weight of my secret. Father, I need confession."

The priest donned his silk stole and entered the confessional.

Moira knelt, protected by the curtain between them, and began, "Bless me, Father. Forgive me for committing a mortal sin."

"I can't imagine you committing a grave offense against God."

She lowered her voice, "Father, I am not pure."

He waited, holding his missal with both hands.

"I've been with a man."

"Moira, God wants you to be chaste until you are married. If you and Paddy..."

She interrupted, "No, Father. Not Paddy."

The priest sat back, "Go on."

She took a deep breath, "I've been forced, Father, against my will. By my employer."

He blessed himself and looked up to his Lord, "Moira, it's not your sin."

"But, I'm not pure."

"Through no fault of your own."

"There's no difference, Father. I'm an Irish Catholic girl. I've lost my virginity. There's no saving me."

"Moira."

"I'm not chaste. Not worthy."

"This is not a measure of your worthiness."

"There's more, Father. Another sin."

He allowed the silence.

"My cousin. When I moved out of the house, he forced himself on her. I knew he would."

"Moira, this problem is bigger than you. You are not responsible for the sins of others."

Tears spilled from her eyes. "I feel such guilt and shame. I'm keeping this secret from Paddy. My cousin is suffering."

"Moira, if it helps take away your guilt, let me give you absolution. You have my word I will find a way to help. You are not the first young woman to bear this burden."

"No one can know."

"There are ways I can help without violating the seal of the confessional. Now go. Find Katie. Comfort each other. One sure way to ease your pain is to reach out to help another."

In his thirty years as a priest, Father Mark listened to hundreds of women confessing sins against purity. Some, like Katie and Moira, were raped by their employer. They confessed, expressing sorrow and shame. They endured their humiliation silently, helpless to defend themselves or leave. Other women, desperate and poor, asked for forgiveness for prostituting themselves to survive and feed their children. When a pregnancy occurred, the women were labeled adulterers and whores.

Father Mark became the rescuer for children born to women who couldn't care for them. Paddy worked in secret with him to place the babies.

He spoke to Paddy, maintaining the confidentiality of Moira's confession. "Son, we've so much work to do. There'll be a knock on my door again. Be sure of it. Another disgraced woman with a baby."

"Father, we do what we can. These women live in despair, hiding their secrets out of shame. Thank the Lord they know enough to turn to you."

"And you. I couldn't help without you. You're to be married. There will come a time Moira will have to know. When do you plan to tell her how you spend the nights you are not home?"

"Aye, not yet. It will lead to more questions."

"About your past?"

Paddy shook his head. "Not sure how she'd take the truth. She assumed I'm from County Clare. I never corrected her. Can't take the chance of losing her."

"She's a fine woman, Paddy. Trust is the foundation of marriage. She loves you. The circumstances of your upbringing won't change that." He tested Paddy, "Is there a secret Moira can tell you to change your love?"

Paddy ended the conversation. "No. There's nothing she can tell me that will stop me from marrying her. I'm off now. You know how to find me."

Moira followed Father Mark's advice and sought Katie out at the park later that week. She offered two daffodils, "Katie please, can we talk?"

Katie grabbed the flowers and threw them. "Why, why do you want to talk now?" She sputtered, "Why didn't you tell me? How could you leave?" Katie pressed her scarlet face into Moira's. She released the fury buried deep within her. "I'm ruined, trapped. It's your fault. Paddy is marrying a fake. You lied to everyone."

The children played in the distance, too far away to hear the explosion.

Moira jumped back, "I'm sorry. Please, let me explain."

Katie raged. She screamed. The robins scattered, "He did it to you. You knew I'd be next, and you, you, never warned me. You just left. Went off to your comfortable new home with your beau. Never caring what happened to me."

"Katie, you don't understand. I thought it was just me. His way of punishing me for being clumsy."

Katie's chest heaved as she tried to breathe.

"Just before I moved out, Cousin Mary told me the English employers see it as their right. I about died. I realized it wasn't just me. Mary told me everything. The English see us as property. Domestics are slaves to them.

They even lend them out to their friends. It's common knowledge, except to us."

Katie countered, "Why didn't you tell me? Warn me?"

"I couldn't admit to it, even to myself. The memory of him crawling on me, probing me…I buried it. The stain of the sin will never fade." Moira wept, "It changed me. I'm ripped apart inside from the guilt of lying to Paddy and leaving you to the same fate."

Rage turned to grief as Katie cried for the first time since the earliest assault. "Moira, please. The shame. I feel so lost, so alone."

Moira wrapped her arms around Katie and rocked her, "You are not alone. You haven't lost me or yourself. You are my sister."

As the two calmed, Moira shared her suspicions. "When I arrived at the Brennan home, Anne, the other nanny had left. There was a newborn, Virginia, and the older two children."

"Yes, that's when you sent me the ticket."

"Mrs. Brennan stayed in her room. She asked after the children when I brought tea."

Katie nodded with understanding.

"Nothing I did was right. I didn't cook or clean the American way. Mr. Brennan ridiculed me for my English. He lashed out at me when I broke his precious dishes and teacups. I cried for home every day. Just before your arrival, he came to my room in the night. I didn't understand. I felt ashamed and dirty. I had no one."

Katie reached for her hand.

"I thought he hated me so much he was punishing me, laying on me, hurting me. I fought him at first. Then I thought I deserved it. The shame was unbearable."

"I wondered why you were moody and hated Mr. Brennan. You told me to lock my door the very first night."

"I lived in fear. If he came to my room in the night, I couldn't breathe the next day. I couldn't lose the memory of him from my mind. You learned faster than I did. I thought you were safe."

Katie responded, "But it wasn't punishment at all."

"I tried to work harder each day. I wanted to please him so he'd leave me alone. I never understood it wasn't about the work."

"Until your cousin Mary told you it's common practice?"

"Yes. I knew then why his wife hid from him. He used Anne, then me, and you were next."

"How many others? Katie mumbled."

Moira looked at her.

"I'm dizzy thinking of the nannies and maids and cooks raped in the dark by their employers."

Moira warned, "We can't speak of it. We have no rights. It's not seen as a crime. The police won't defend Irish girls over an English man. We will be shamed and seen as whores."

Katie and Moira sat in silence, their faces swollen and blotched from crying. Exhausted after unleashing their emotions, they watched the children play.

The afternoon passed and the early spring air cooled. Moira did not confide to Katie that she had confessed to Father Mark. She reminded her, "Our whole lives we've been taught to stay pure for our wedding night. We must suffer this shame in silence."

"Aye," Katie replied. "We won't be forgiven by the Church for impurity. No good man will take us for a wife."

"Our *lives* will be ruined by scandal. We'll be known as sinners in the Catholic Church that forbids a man and woman to be together before marriage. Our families will reject us. What will become of us?"

Katie dared ask, "Moira, could I become pregnant?"

Moira responded without taking a breath. "Aye, and there's no secret then. If it happens to us, we'll be left begging with a baby in the streets."

"In Ireland, they send the girls away for years."

"Aye. Please God, you won't meet that fate."

"We must keep this to ourselves. I have to find a way out."

"Perhaps a job in a shop, and a respectable room to rent. I will make inquiries. Try to smile more," Moira chided, "Maybe you'll meet a lad."

A glint came to Katie's eye. She leaned toward her cousin. "Yes, Moira, I'll pretty myself up and attract a lad."

The children spied Moira and shrieked with joy. She kissed and hugged each one, swinging them around. "Children are so innocent."

"My happy escape," Katie agreed, pressing Virginia to her chest.

They left the park bound by their secret. The daffodils wilted on the ground. "Moira, it is a sin in the Catholic Church to be with a man before marriage."

"Paddy never questioned me. He assumes I am a virgin."

"And the virgin's stain on the bedclothes?"

Moira turned to Katie, looking older than her twenty-one years. "There will be blood. Not from me, from the butcher's meat. It will be the last deception between me and Paddy."

Chapter 8
MARRIAGE

BOSTON MASSACHUSETS

SPRING 1870...Paddy held Moira's hands, looked at her and whispered, "A-suilish mahuilagus machre," then, "light of my eyes and my heart." His voice cracked and his face flushed red as he asked her to marry him, "Dean a suas a'mhairiste leam?"

They stood on the banks of the Charles River where they spent many hours of their courtship. It was there they discussed the importance of honesty and trust between husband and wife. During those first months, Moira was giddy. As time went on she became more serious and sometimes distant. Paddy wanted more, "Moira, I'm asking for your trust. There is sadness in your eyes. I want to take it away. Will you let me?"

Moira struggled, "What if I can't be what you want in a wife, Paddy? I don't want to disappoint you."

"You can't disappoint me. I wish you saw yourself as I do."

"There is so much I care about."

"That's why I love you. We both want to work to make a better life for ourselves and others. I love that you're thoughtful and kind. I love your smile and laugh and how your red hair curls in the rain. Imagine us together forever and blessed with lovely children. Do you want that?"

"I do, yes, I do."

Paddy reassured, "Take my hand. Open your heart. Walk with me into our future. I'll be a good and caring husband and we will grow old together. You will be a loving wife and mother for our children. There is nothing to fear with me by your side."

Paddy's commitment to Moira did not take away her fears. Father Mark's absolution forgave the sin against God, but did not restore her virginity or relieve the shame or guilt of hiding her secret. Father Mark counseled her to share her secret with Paddy. "Marriage is based on trust and honesty. You and Paddy have discussed this. Trust that Paddy will understand."

"I won't, Father. Paddy is deeply devoted to the Catholic Church. I won't risk asking him to make a choice between his faith and marrying an impure woman."

"I understand, Moira. But I wish you had more faith in Paddy."

Over months of courtship, Paddy's patience and consistent devotion helped Moira open her heart. When he first declared his love, she responded without hesitation. "I am so thankful for you, Paddy. You have my undying love."

And now, Easter Sunday, springtime in Boston, and Paddy McMahon and Moira Murphy pledged their intentions. Paddy presented Moira with a Claddagh ring. "Two hands hold the heart that is ours. This ring is a symbol of friendship, love and loyalty between us."

"I love you, Paddy. God's blessed me with you. You are a gift. More than I deserve." Paddy slipped the ring on the third finger of her right hand with the top of the crown facing away from her heart. "When we say our marriage vows, I'll place this ring on your left hand, with the crown facing your heart." They embraced for the first time as an engaged couple. Paddy shielded Moira, protecting her from the chill of the wind off the water.

The Flynn home teemed with well-wishers. Guests made toasts, told jokes, and recounted stories of ill-fated marriage proposals.

Mrs. Flynn hosted a garden party. Dressed in her Easter Sunday clothes, she greeted each guest. Declan shook hands and accepted congratulations due the bride's father. Father Mark quieted the revelers and offered a blessing. "May the good Lord bring you love, life and happiness."

Friends enjoyed a ham dinner, with buttered potatoes, beets, and turnip. The party lasted into the night. Fiddlers played, and whiskey and Guinness flowed in celebration of the happy couple.

Moira and Katie slipped away and hugged with joy. Moira was engaged to marry 'the most handsome lad in Boston,' as she dubbed him at first sight. Katie cared for Paddy, but never fancied him as handsome. At their first meeting, she thought, *Oh, my. This man cannot tame his hair. His chin is chiseled to a point.* His wide smile captured her. *His grin reaches each of his large ears and invites you to him. Yes, he is a match for Moira.*

The two planned to meet in the park during the week. "We've talked about this day for so long. We'll surely be able to make final plans in time for a June wedding."

"I have ideas for your dress and flowers, and of course, the food."

"Mary will sew the dress. We spoke with Father Mark, and he will marry us. Oh, our dreams are coming true. This will be a happy time for us, at last."

Katie forced a smile and thought, *Happy for you, Moira. What's to become of me?*

Wedding preparations consumed Moira's thoughts and time. She did not fulfill her promise to find a respectable sales position or boarding house for Katie. Once she and Katie renewed their friendship and Paddy proposed, the bounce in her step returned. She buried their shared secret once again.

Katie hinted, "Will you be keeping your job after the marriage?"

"For a while. Once I'm with child, I'll be leaving."

Katie tried again. "Would be grand if we worked together. You know, so I can leave Mr. Brennan."

The smile fell from Moira's face. "Katie, I'm sorry. Forgive me. I've been so taken with plans." She reached for her cousin.

Katie cried, "Please, don't forget me. You're my only hope. It's over for you, but not for me. I pray every night for God to send me a way out."

———

Preparations for the wedding began. Mary bought a piece of blue silk. "I'll fit the bodice to you at the waist. The skirt will flow to the floor. We'll make the seams extra wide, and take them out when you're with child. After the wedding, this will be your special occasion dress."

"I'm imagining myself a bride, dressed in blue silk."

"A crinoline will make the dress more bridal."

Mary finished stitching and brought out a piece of Irish lace. "I thought I'd use this lace for a christening dress for my own children..." her voice faded. "You are a daughter to me, so today, Moira, I'll fashion your wedding dress with a lace collar and cuffs."

Moira teared up. "And you've been a mother to me."

Paddy and Moira completed plans. As the day approached, Moira assured Paddy of her love. "It will be the first day of the rest of our lives together."

Katie appeared with fresh flowers the day of the wedding. "I've made a braid for your hair and a bouquet for you to carry."

"Thank you, my dear Katie. You are so sweet."

"And of course, every bride must have a magic hanky. I crocheted an Irish cross on it. Tuck it into your wedding dress. It's a sign of fertility. With just a few stitches, it will make a fine christening bonnet for your first child."

"And you will be Godmother."

Bagpipes called the guests to attention. Paddy gasped at the vision in blue. His bride had the face of an angel framed in red ringlets. Her cheeks blushed in soft rose. He whispered aloud, "I love you," despite instructions from Father Mark to let him do the talking.

The priest welcomed the couple and guests. His sermon described Paddy's devotion to his faith. He praised him for his commitment to the community as a fireman, and now to his bride. He spoke of the bride. "Moira left Ireland as a young girl to find a better life in America. Today she is a woman, stronger now for the sacrifices she made." He and Moira exchanged a knowing glance.

He blessed them as they pledged to love and honor one another. "And may the good Lord bless you with children."

Moira dabbed tears with the handkerchief.

Father Mark ended the ceremony with the Irish tradition of 'tying the knot.' He wrapped a string around the couple's clasped hands and tied it.

"Go forward. In the eyes of God, love each other. You are bonded forever by the marriage vows you pledged today."

The wedding celebration lasted into the next day. Men gathered on one side of the church hall and sang and drank the night away. Women brought plates of ham and corned beef, cabbage, potatoes, carrots and peas. The feast continued with Irish soda bread and sherry trifle. Mary made a traditional Irish wedding fruitcake, filled with almonds, raisins, and cherries, and spiced with brandy.

Tears flowed when Declan read a letter from Moira's mother and father.

Our Dearest Moira,
Our hearts are withe ye today as you pledge youre love and faidelity.
May the good Lord bless and keep ye in the palm of His hand.
Your luving Mam and Da

Paddy's fellow firemen reveled in toasting him and telling stories. One described Paddy as a man of integrity and deep faith. The wedding guests laughed when he warned, "Now, you must be a patient and obliging husband, so as not to ignite the fiery temper inside all red-headed women."

Paddy lifted his glass in agreement.

The toast continued, "I'm gifting you this wedding bell. Place it top your hearth. When an argument begins, ring it. It will remind you of the commitment you made today."

The guests roared and raised their glasses.

The stories continued. Fireman Michael O'Connor regaled the guests, "I've got a wonderful friend, Danny Sullivan, married to a lovely girl. Now I noticed Danny called his wife, 'Darlin', even after thirty-five years of marriage. So one day I asked him, 'Danny,' I said, 'how is it you call your wife darlin' even after such a long marriage?'

'Well,' said my friend, 'I forgot her real name fifteen years ago, so it's all I have.'" The guests laughed and clapped as more Irish stories unfolded.

Later, when the dancing resumed, Father Mark signaled Paddy. They walked outside. "I'm sorry to interrupt the festivities, Paddy, but I'll be needing your help in a few days."

"Of course, Father. Moira and I are not going on a honeymoon just yet. Tell me. Who is it that needs our help?"

Father Mark checked to confirm they were alone. "A young woman, a Negro, came to my door yesterday. She's a scrubwoman in a factory and ready to give birth."

"Raped?"

Father Mark lowered his voice, "I don't know. She's hidden the pregnancy from everyone. Came to me after she heard of the Catholic priest who gave another woman rent money."

"Where is she now?"

"Working. She's not Catholic. Took a big chance asking for help from a priest. Didn't know if she could trust me."

"What did you say?"

"I've made arrangements for her to go to the midwife when the pains come."

"And then?"

"We'll do as we've done in the past. One of the women who've agreed to wet nurse our infants will take the child for a few days. The mother doesn't want the child. We'll take it to the Sisters in Lowell."

"The orphanage?"

"Paddy, we cannot judge. She can't keep it. A Negro woman with a baby won't get a job. They'll be on the street."

"Can you place it with a family?"

Father Mark nodded, "I've tried. The Negroes are too poor. They can't feed their own."

"I suppose the orphanage is best. At least the Sisters will teach it to read and write and give it a clean place to live."

Father Mark placed his hand on Paddy's shoulder. "Now go back to your wife, son. I'll let you know when to bring the carriage. Should be soon."

Paddy returned to his wedding celebration distracted now by the story of the young Negro woman. He found the guests linked arm and arm, singing Irish tunes. Joining in, he wrapped his arm around his wife's waist, kissing her head. "We are so blessed. I thank God you never suffered the evils of this world."

Moira did not respond, but leaned into her new husband.

"Come, little one, I want to be alone with you."

Katie broke from the singing to bid the couple goodbye. "This has been a grand day. I lost myself in the music."

"It's the wedding we've planned for years. I thank you. I would not have married without you here with me."

They hugged and Paddy joined, pulling the three closer.

The exhausted newlyweds spent the night in their new home. They made love for the first time. A sweet, gentle and new love.

"Is tum o ghra."

"I love you, too, Paddy."

Paddy woke the next morning to find blood-stained bedclothes.

Katie returned to 2102 Beacon Street before dawn. She climbed the stairs to the children's rooms and checked Virginia. As she entered the older children's room, her eyes adjusted to the light from the moon. They focused on a figure sitting in the rocking chair.

Chapter 9
MEET ROSE BRENNAN

BOSTON MASSACHUSETTS

SUMMER 1870...The fragile silhouette in the moonlight was Rose Brennan. She sat in a white, flowing nightdress. Gentle waves of light brown hair draped her neck and shoulders.

Katie hadn't seen Mrs. Brennan out of bed. She'd glimpsed her when delivering tea and meals to a darkened room. "Mrs. Brennan. Sorry, mum."

A soft, delicate voice responded. "It's all right, Katie. I sometimes sit and watch my children and wonder what they are dreaming."

She called me by name.

"Shall I go, mum, and leave you to the children?"

"That's not necessary. I'll be retiring to my room. Perhaps you'll bring tea and tell me about the wedding."

The wedding! What else does she know!

"Yes, mum, surely. Let me fetch you tea."

"Katie, bring yourself a cup as well."

Jesus, Jesus, God save me. Tea with Mrs. Brennan.

"Yes, of course, mum. If you say so."

Still wearing Mrs. Brennan's hand-me-down frock, Katie rushed to the kitchen to boil water. Hands shaking, thoughts raced through her mind. *Mrs. Brennan, out of her room...looking at the wee ones. Did this happen often?* Trying not to break another English bone china saucer, she gathered cups and plates. *Calm yourself, girl, this is a chance to learn what goes on in this house.*

Katie moved quietly about the house. She reached the room without dropping a cup. Her eyes scanned the dark wood furniture, a dressing table with reflecting glass, a chest of drawers and the bed. Leaving her shoes at the door, her feet touch a soft, thick, green patterned carpet.

Mrs. Brennan sat propped by pillows in her four-poster bed. "Thank you, Katie. Are you too tired to stay and tell me about the wedding? I'm sure Moira made a lovely bride."

"Oh, yes, mum. And Paddy, a handsome groom, as well."

Mrs. Brennan gestured to a chair by the bed. Katie chatted on, giving Mrs. Brennan all the details of the courtship and wedding celebration. "Moira glowed with joy as she joined Paddy at the altar."

"And what did Moira wear?"

"Oh, Mrs. Brennan. The loveliest blue silk dress. Her cousin Mary sewed it. Blue is the traditional color for Irish brides."

"Is that so?"

"And she carried a magic hanky, another tradition. I crocheted it myself. It will make the christening bonnet for their first child."

"And the groom? Who is he?"

"Paddy McMahon, a fireman. Moira fancies him the most handsome lad in Boston. He's not to my taste. His nose and chin come to a point. His hair is a tangle of brown curls about his whole head."

Mrs. Brennan laughed at Katie's description. "Well, what's inside is more important than a pointy chin and untamed hair." Her smile and warm voice differed from the cranky, cold, recluse Katie imagined.

"He's a fine lad, Mrs. Brennan. His smile draws you to him, and his eyes, blue as the sea."

"Moira deserves happiness. I wished her good fortune when she moved to her cousin's home."

"Was it sad to lose her? The children love Moira."

"Sad, yes, for me and the children, but best for Moira."

They chatted until sunrise. "Mrs. Brennan, I've got to be going to start my work."

"Please, Katie, will you visit again? I want to hear more about the children and how they spend their days. Charles and Margaret are growing so fast. It pains me to miss their childhoods."

"Of course, mum. The children are wonderful. They are happy and quite bright. I read them The New England Primer. We are learning together. And Virginia is darlin'. A little heart breaker, that one is."

Mrs. Brennan's smile faded at the mention of Virginia. Katie thought, *Well, you've done it now. After the birth of Virginia, she took to the bed and closed the drapes. Now you've just brought her up.*

Katie backed out of the room, empty tea cups in hand. "I'll surely be back another time with reports of the children. I'll bring us tea."

The pre-dawn visits continued throughout the summer and into the fall. Mrs. Brennan opened the drapes allowing the moonlight into the room. She sat in bed, wearing a pressed breakfast coat over her nightdress. Conversations centered on the children's lives. The chats led to a warm friendship. Mrs. Brennan warned, "Mr. Brennan must never learn of our visits. He can't know of the nights I sit in the rocker watching the children sleep."

Katie nodded in agreement.

"I take walks at night as well. It helps me to breathe in the fresh air. We will both pay a high price if Mr. Brennan knows about our time together. He's not a tolerant man."

Katie tried to open a door, "Why do you suppose he is not tolerant?"

"Oh, my love, it is such a long story. As for you, Mr. Brennan is among the English who despise Irish Catholics. They see them as stupid, drunken fools. He thinks he'd be lowering himself to speak to you. He forbade me to hire another Irish girl to replace Moira."

"Aye, he hired Etta."

"He thinks he got his way. The truth is, I didn't want to bring another young girl to this house. My hope is he has no interest in a large, older, Colored." Mrs. Brennan continued without a pause. "He hired Etta because he prefers a black woman over an Irish one. He hates the Coloreds, except for William. That's how little he thinks of the Irish. He doesn't see you as an equal human being, but as his dispensable property."

Hot rods shot through Katie's brain. She jumped up. Her teacup dropped to the carpet. "Dispensable property...not an equal human being. What is he but a selfish, cruel man?"

Mrs. Brennan remained calm and extended her pale white hand to Katie. "You don't understand the English views of the Irish. It's not just about you and Mr. Brennan. The English have used the Irish as their servant race for centuries."

Katie's hands trembled. She retrieved the cup from the floor. She was screaming inside. *Oh, yes, it is about me and Mr. Brennan. He's using me and will throw me away when he's finished. My life is his dispensable property.*

Katie composed herself and reported on the reading and writing progress of Margaret and Charles. "Charles enjoys numbers problems and tries until he's solved each one. Margaret loves to sing and read stories." She didn't mention Mr. Brennan or Virginia.

During a chat in late fall, Mrs. Brennan asked about suitors. "You're a lovely woman, Katie. How many young men are asking to court you?"

"That would be none, Mrs. Brennan. I seldom leave the house. Biding my time to return to Galway."

"The day will come for you. A handsome lad will win your heart."

Katie proceeded with caution, "Did you enjoy your courtship with Mr. Brennan?"

The question lingered as the two women sat with their tea. Mrs. Brennan in her bed, Katie in the chair next to her. Mrs. Brennan looked at Katie, glanced away and sighed. Katie waited. "We had a different courtship than most," she started. "Mr. Brennan was twenty-seven and I, twenty-five. We were both past marrying age."

"Why does age make a courtship different?"

"Well, as one gets older, there are fewer suitors. Single women don't have many options for work and respectable living arrangements. And if you want children, you might both...compromise."

"So, you married Mr. Brennan, but didn't love him?"

Mrs. Brennan maintained her soft voice and in her lilting English accent went on. "I never said I didn't love him when we married. I did have a kind of love for him. He first saw me in the millinery shop where I worked after my father died."

"I'm sorry about your father."

"Yes, we left England together for a new life. My father raised me alone after my mother passed. A physician, he wanted to minister to the poor English in America. I was to run his office, a secure position for a single woman. He died the first winter we were here." Mrs. Brennan sipped her tea. "A true irony. The doctor couldn't save himself from the dysentery he acquired on the trip over."

"It must have been hard for you to be alone. Like me."

"I didn't plan to marry. But my father's estate was meager. Enough for me to live simply for a few years." She paused, "As a woman alone, it became a necessity."

"Is that why you married Mr. Brennan? Because you were alone?"

"Well, no. Not entirely. Mr. Brennan tried to win me. He did his best to be attentive and charming. He learned my first name and came to the shop with a rose. He presented it, 'A rose for a Rose'."

"That doesn't sound like Mr. Brennan."

"He was kind at first." Mrs. Brennan glanced at her dresser. "He gave me that jewelry box as a wedding gift. Open it."

Katie walked to the dresser and picked up the carved cherry wood box. She lifted the top to expose a silk rose-colored lining.

A faint smile crossed Mrs. Brennan's face, "He said it reminded him of me. His attention helped me recover from the loss of my father. I didn't understand he saw me as one of his possessions. He wanted a wife to bring value to his life. At first he impressed me with his hard work and ambition until I saw it was driven by greed."

Katie looked confused.

"I've often wondered what my father would have advised me. He raised me as an equal to men. There is no equality in marriage. The role of the wife is to produce children, be dutiful to her husband and comply to his rules."

"Yet, you chose to marry."

"I thought all men were like my father. He treated me as a person with ideas and opinions. I didn't understand that once married, a woman lost her identity and even rights. The law is applied based on men's views."

"Why do you stay married?"

"There's no choice. Divorced women have no rights to their children or their husband's property. I haven't worked since we married. Even during the Civil War when many women took jobs, he insisted I stay at home."

Katie asked about Mr. Brennan's past. "Does he have family?"

"No, his parents abandoned him as a young boy, around Charles' age. He was poorer than the most destitute of the Irish."

"And he despises the poor Irish?"

"He does. Mr. Brennan sees himself as a success. He suffered at the hands of others for the first ten years of his life. And then he sacrificed and worked day and night to become wealthy. It's not just the Irish, he hates all people. He only has love for his possessions."

"Does he love the children?"

"If he could love like other people, he would love them. Because of the way he is, he sees them as his possessions, like me and you. He'll let no harm come to them. They won't suffer as he did. I believe that."

At this point, the sun came up. Katie excused herself. "Mrs. Brennan, I must leave to prepare for the day. May I hear more of the story another time?"

"Rose, please, call me Rose. And close the drapes before you go. Thank you, Katie." Mrs. Brennan pulled the covers up and leaned her head on the pillow.

"Sorry, mum. Did it upset you to talk about Mr. Brennan?"

"I'm afraid it did, Katie. My life is so full of regrets. It makes me very sad when I talk about it."

Chapter 10
CHARLES BRENNAN

BOSTON MASSACHUSETTS

SPRING 1870...I'm not a man born of privilege. My first memory as a child is being cold, wet and hungry. A terrible feeling, being hungry. At ten years old, my home was the streets of London. My bed, the dirt alleys. I stole what I needed. Sometimes from other street boys. It was a means of survival. My companions were stray mutts, who like me, didn't belong to anyone.

My name isn't even Brennan. No need for a name on the streets. No one talks to you. When I got put into a poorhouse, they said I had to have one. I remembered being called Charles by a woman, maybe my mother. It's my only memory of her, that and the smell of whiskey on her breath. The people at the poorhouse decided to call me Charles Brennan, because an orphan named Brennan just died and didn't need the name. The garbage I found on the streets was better than the food at the poorhouse. Meals were mush. The matrons beat me almost every day. Each time I ran away, they brought me back and lashed me again. Every kid was crawling with lice and scratching from bed bugs. They kept us busy scrubbing floors and washing pots over and over. Rain or sun, hot or cold, each day we stood outside for an hour.

Before long I got shipped off to Montreal, Canada. The government decided us orphans might be of more use as slaves on livestock ranches. We were supposed to go to school to learn how to herd cattle.

They promised clothes and food and comfortable passage. Only orphans who read and wrote and were sixteen or older were supposed to go. In the end, it didn't matter. If you were an orphan or at least unclaimed, on the ship you went.

I was ten. They put five hundred of us, all boys, in the hold of the ship. We were crowded in with the cattle. It was vermin infested, stinking and dark all the time. We slept on the floor, puking from the rocking of the ship. We shit in our clothes. Some couldn't take it, and died. I watched naked bodies being hoisted out of the hold. The older boys stripped them for the clothes.

The trip lasted weeks. I lost track of time. We were hot and starving. The big boys took their rage out on the youngest. I was small, and an easy target. They beat me every day. The meanest stripped me naked and sodomized me with the handle of the water ladle. They made sport of me. I stopped fighting back because they just hit me harder when I did. Tried to hide, but it was no use. No one helped. They were grateful it was me and not them. By the time we reached Canada, I had no front teeth and was deaf in my right ear from so many bangs on the head.

The beatings made me strong and angry. I wasn't about to become a slave for a rancher. I planned to be on my own again. We were being loaded onto a train to Ontario. That's when I made my break. I ran. It was spring and easy to survive in warm weather. I hopped trains. Slept in the forest. Ate berries and bugs when I had to. But I was free. No one was beating me, and no one would ever again.

I made my way to Middlebury, Vermont. It was fall and turning cold. I found a woodshop and snuck in after dark to sleep. At first I thought the owner didn't notice me. I used a pile of sawdust for a bed and ate scraps he threw out for the dog. After a few nights, a blanket appeared and some cheese and bread. Mr. Hasty was the first kind person I ever met. He didn't talk much, but gave me chores to earn my keep. I swept floors and kept the wood burning stove hot. He let me watch him work.

Hasty was a master craftsman, creating custom bowls, spoons and cutting boards. He made larger items like gun racks, bed frames and chairs.

His dining tables and breakfronts were crafted of white pine with satin-wood veneers and custom jigsaw work. The only time he talked was to explain his craft to me.

He encouraged me to travel around Vermont to learn techniques of master craftsmen who used exotic woods like rosewood and walnut. I went to Woodstock, Rutland and Bennington. I memorized each maker's mark. I watched as they worked the color and grain of local woods to create veneers with their signature patterns. They used tiger maple and yellow birch, and etched fine lines and carved ornamentation to call attention to a piece.

After four years of study, I understood the nuances of woods like cherry, mahogany and oak. I recognized the work of individual woodworkers and the value of the intricacies of their work.

I returned to Mr. Hasty in Middlebury. His furniture was known in Boston, and he willingly filled orders for custom Mission style and Colonial furniture. His walking sticks were in high demand, as were his hand-carved musical instruments. Times were changing in the cities. New immigrants were ready to give up the musty furnishings they brought from the old country. They were modernizing with handcrafted American styles.

Mr. Hasty engaged me to deliver his unique, modern pieces to wealthy customers in Boston. Each time I made a delivery, I graciously offered to remove old furniture no longer wanted in the home. I asked questions, the year it was made, craftsman or artist, country of origin. I accepted furnishings that no longer fit the modern décor, four French antique copper plated engravings from the 1700s, an English pewter teapot with a Tudor rose and crown, an Italian gold, gilded mirror, a set of French porcelain cachepots. I soon had a collection of others' treasured family heirlooms from around the world.

I used my meager earnings to rent a small storefront on the north side of Boston and placed my belongings there. In time, I left Vermont and lived in the storefront, surrounded by my treasures. I slept on the floor, covered by the blanket from the woodshop. At fifteen, for the first time in my life, I had possessions. My own possessions.

I spent the next ten years bartering, buying and selling. I scoured streets for abandoned furniture. I took the velvet upholstery from a useless sofa and saved a chair. For the first few years I continued to eat from others' garbage, never spending my money when food was readily available.

I studied. Asked questions. By the time I was twenty-five my business included imports from the Orient, Italy, and India. I saved every penny and purchased a four-story brownstone row house with a large first floor storefront. I commissioned a fine, tailored black suit for conducting business, and lived among the wealthy Brahmins. They sought me out for my knowledge and expertise in fine furnishings, carpets and art. I got rich from their money.

In spite of the trappings of a home in a prestigious section of Boston, custom business suit, and new wealth, I was still the poor boy, abandoned on the streets of London. My Cockney accent, unmistakable. My manners, wanting. I had yet to earn the respect of my neighbors. And then I met the perfect addition to my collection.

Rose is a fine specimen of a proper English woman. She's from upper class, the daughter of a physician, fairly educated and speaks the Queen's English. Like a dainty piece of Chinese porcelain, she's refined in her dress and looks, with delicate features, pure white skin and silky brown hair.

As luck would have it, Rose's father died and left her alone in the world. She couldn't survive as a single woman in Boston. We were both past marrying age and willing to make compromises. The courtship was swift. Assuming a lonely spinster craved male attention, I presented her with a rose and said it reminded me of her. As expected, her face lit up. Within months, I offered her a jewelry box, lined with rose-colored silk, as an enticement to marry me. I didn't want to prolong the courtship for no good reason. It worked. Rose agreed to the marriage. And why not? I was rich and offered her a home furnished with fine antiques, selected by me personally. All she had to do was produce the children. We seemed a perfect match. My life was complete, a home, wealth, possessions, and now with Rose, respectability.

I'm Charles Brennan, a self-made man. I may not have the manners and accent of a Boston Brahmin, but hard work earned me the money and the right to live on Beacon Hill.

Chapter 11
PRAYING FOR A MIRACLE

BOSTON MASSACHUSETTS

JUNE 1870…Paddy arrived at Father Mark's quarters. "It's after midnight. I've been praying for you, Paddy. I assume the baby is safe in the hands of the Sisters in Lowell."

"Aye, Father. A long ride for a newborn. He did well. The Sisters are taking good care of him. How's the mother?"

Father Mark tamped ashes from his pipe, "She's suffering, son. I've seen too much of this in my years in Boston."

"You're doing what you can to help these young women. Where would they turn without you?"

"And you and the women who wet nurse the infants. I don't do this alone. But I'm discouraged, Paddy. There's been no progress. I've been ministering to desperately poor immigrants for almost three decades. Even in the years since the famine, thousands left Ireland for Boston only to find themselves living in crowded, squalid conditions. So many lives lost to disease and drink. Babies are born to live just long enough to die and leave heartbroken mothers."

Paddy nodded, "Aye, Father. The Irish have suffered for hundreds of years. Seems it's their lot. They've gone from starvation and oppression in Ireland to America, where they are shunned and hated. Many a man's been driven to despair, for sure."

Father Mark's face reflected his worry. "I don't know, Paddy. I'm losing hope."

"Father, I've watched the Irish population in Boston over the years. There's no denying it's been hard, but they are better off today than when you came over. So many, especially the women, turn to the Church for the strength and courage to go on. You are the heart and soul of our community. You have to believe that."

The priest, balding and stout after decades of working for the poor, offered a smile. "Thank you, Paddy. I hope my fifty-five years on earth haven't been in vain. I wish we could do more."

"Father, we have no money."

"Aye, and now, since the war, we've men in hospitals, sick and maimed. We help one soldier or a desperate woman, while hundreds go with no help."

"You can't do it all, Father. You are one man."

"I haven't been sleeping, Paddy. We have to find a way to do more, son."

"Aye, I'm here to help. Do you have a plan?"

He stood from his chair and put his arm on Paddy's shoulder, "I do. Let me talk to the Lord. Then I'll let you in on it. For now, go home to your lovely wife."

Father Mark tried to sleep. Images of the suffering poor plagued him. He thought of Moira, Katie, the young Colored mother, and the other women he could only help after their abuse. At dawn, he rose from his bed to craft a letter.

His hands trembled as he focused on each word.

June, 1870

Dearest Sister Mary Bernadette,

I commend you on the work the Sisters of Mercy did on the battlefields during the Civil War. The bravery and fortitude of the Sisters saved the lives of thousands of men.

I'm aware of the exemplary work your Order does training others in nursing techniques you developed on the battlefield for sanitation, wound care, and treatment of cholera and dysentery. The improvements in care at St. Peter's Hospital of Philadelphia are widely documented. I pray you will continue your work.

I pray, also, Sister, for the people of Boston. We have many poor and suffering. Our almshouses are filled beyond capacity with the sick and wounded. I do what I can to relieve the spiritual suffering of these poor souls. I cannot, however, fill the need for proper nursing care for their bodies.

At the same time, there is little respectable work for young immigrant women. Some suffer a multitude of abuses at the hands of their employers. Others toil long hours in inhumane conditions.

After weeks of contemplation and prayer, I'm convinced your presence in Boston, training young women as nurses, will bring relief to the social issues the Irish and other immigrants face. Women trained in your nursing techniques will offer improved healthcare to our sick and elderly.

There is an abandoned schoolhouse on parish grounds. It will provide the ideal setting to train nurses. However, the building is in need of repair. We are a poor parish and look to you for the ten thousand dollars needed to replace the roof and ready the building. I pray the Sisters will come to Boston and offer nurses' training once the renovation is complete.

Please consider my request. I strongly believe our partnership will bring blessings and new hope to the Boston Catholic community.

I look forward to your response.

God Bless You,

Father Mark Boyle

Father Mark shared his plan with Paddy. "The letter is mailed. Now, we wait and pray."

"That's a grand plan, Father. Moira will help, I'm sure. Right now, she's focused on conceiving a child. It's all she talks about."

"Keep praying, Paddy. A child for you and a mission for Boston."

It was six months, almost Christmas, when the response arrived. Father Mark blessed himself and read.

> *December, 1870*
> *Blessings, Father Mark,*
> *The Sisters of Mercy are in receipt of your request. We currently of-fer nurses' training and housing missions in New York and Philadelphia. Our experience on the battlefields allowed us to develop safe and sterile nursing techniques, which improved the survival rate for wounded sol-diers and the sick in hospitals and at home.*
>
> *Many of our students are young immigrant women. The housing we provide offers them a haven, and the training, an opportunity for employment.*
>
> *Major cities across the country are asking our Sisters to train nurses to aid the sick and dying. We prayed for guidance regarding your request for the Sisters of Mercy to establish such a mission in Boston.*
>
> *Regrettably…*

Oh, Dear God, they are turning me down, Father Mark raised his head and whispered a prayer.

> *…at this time, the Sisters do not have the financial resources to ren-ovate your building. We pray you will secure the ten thousand dollars needed for the mission and school supplies.*
>
> *Please contact me when the project is complete and we will send a number of Sisters to assist you.*
> *God Bless You,*
> *Sister Mary Bernadette, SM*

He read the letter again. *There is hope, but my parishioners are poor. It will take a miracle to raise the money.*

Father Mark addressed the parishioners at every Sunday Mass. "Many of our men, wounded and sick, lay in hospitals. Good volunteers care for them, and we are grateful."

He appealed to them, "These men often die from infection due to unsanitary conditions and lack of nursing care, not from their wounds."

Father Mark had the attention of his flock. "We have the opportunity to bring proper nursing care to Boston. The Sisters of Mercy will establish a mission on parish property. Here, women of Boston will live and train as nurses. They will work in our hospitals and bring nursing care to your homes.

"We need ten thousand dollars to renovate the building and furnish the school. Let us pray God will show us the way."

Parishioners deposited pennies in the basket at the back of the church. "Paddy, we'll not be seeing ten thousand dollars from the pockets of our people. We have to find a wealthy donor."

Paddy embraced the challenge. "Father, I have an idea. I'll need a letter from you requesting a donation." He brought the letter and his charm to an Irish councilman. "Councilman Walsh, thank you for your efforts to improve the lot of the Boston Irish, especially the fire and policemen. I'm sure a man of your status has the ears of Irish businessmen in Boston." Paddy offered his wide grin and a wink to Councilman Walsh. "I've come to you only, sir, to give you the opportunity to further endear yourself to Boston voters." He continued, with all the charm he could summon, "If you pass this letter along, I'm betting a wealthy businessman will leap at the chance to train Boston women in proper nursing techniques. The training will educate our women and prepare them for respectable work. As if that is not enough, Councilman Walsh, Boston will offer better health care to our brave soldiers and sick citizens. It's a grand effort."

Councilman Walsh did not respond.

Paddy offered the letter and added, "Philadelphia and New York already offer nurses' training and modern healthcare techniques developed by the good Sisters."

The Councilman raised an eyebrow. "Is that a fact?"

"You, of course, will be recognized as the Councilman responsible for bringing this blessing to Boston."

That might be too much blarney, even from me, Paddy thought to himself.

Councilman Walsh accepted the letter and shook hands with Paddy. "I'll see what I can do, son."

Months passed. No benefactor appeared.

Paddy confided his disappointment to his wife, "I can't believe it. Not one man has stepped up. I thought we'd have the money in hand by now."

Moira feigned sympathy for Paddy's disappointment. "You deserve it, Paddy. You worked hard convincing Councilman Walsh."

"I'm sorry, luv, I shouldn't be carryin' on about my problems. I know you are more concerned about the miscarriages. Two in ten months… I wish I could make you feel better."

Moira wore her feelings of worthlessness on her face and in her posture. They were apparent to those who knew her best. Father Mark reached out, "Moira, is there anything I can do to help?"

"No, Father, this is a burden I must bear alone. My shame keeps me from bearing a child." She looked at him, "Perhaps prayers."

"You are always in my prayers, child. I pray you'll be relieved of the pain of your past."

Moira swallowed at the reference to her secret. Holding his gaze into her eyes, he continued, "I left Ireland to serve the Irish immigrants in Boston. I've listened to dozens of young women who suffered at the hands of their employer."

Moira lowered her head, "I've carried this secret for so long."

"I know. The shame is great. I've been awakened many times in the middle of the night to find a young woman at my door holding a newborn infant in her arms."

"What happens to them?"

"The women or the infants? If there is no family willing to take in a child, I bring the infants to an orphanage. Sometimes the father, if he's an English employer, makes a grand gesture and adopts the child without acknowledging it as his own."

"And the women?"

"In my many years as a priest, they are my greatest sadness."

"Tell me, Father."

"The shame, guilt and loss are often too great. Abandoning a child, not knowing where they are, who they are with, is all too much."

Moira's eyes widened.

"They often take to drink or the street life. Some are lost forever. Others find the strength to move on."

Moira moved from thoughts of herself, "What can we do?"

"Right now, we pray for a miracle. I cannot violate the seal of the confessional, but I also won't stand by without trying to stop the abuse."

"I want to help, but I won't risk others knowing about me."

"Moira, dear, there are ways to help without revealing your secrets. You and Paddy are well known in the parish. You might help raise the money for the nursing school. And later, the Sisters will call upon you to influence women to take the training. It's good work."

He reached for her hand, "It may help distract you."

"Yes, Father, I need that. Tell me what to do."

Father tilted his head and spoke in his finest Irish brogue, "Could you conjure a miracle for us, Mrs. McMahon?"

Moira smiled.

"We need ten thousand dollars. If you can't bring us a miracle, perhaps you'll enlist Katie and Paddy to pray with us."

"Of course, Father. Please, remember, Katie cannot know I confided in you that she, too, is suffering at the hands of Mr. Brennan. It's not for me to share her secret shame."

"I understand. Now, go and start praying."

Moira waited until after Mass to tell Katie the news. "We need ten thousand dollars to start the school. The Sisters will help once we have the building ready."

"At last, Moira, this is my future, a nurse."

They walked together, enjoying the spring air, "Father Mark wants your prayers. It may take a miracle to raise the ten thousand dollars."

"Of course. I hope He hears them."

Moira couldn't hold back, "Pray for me, too. I just want a baby." She cried to Katie, "I didn't even tell Paddy I missed my monthly again. I don't want him to know I lost another baby."

Katie listened, as always. "Try to stay calm. So much crying isn't good for you."

"God's punishing me for my sins. I know He is."

"You are burdening yourself with guilt. Talk with Father Mark. Ask forgiveness for whatever sins you have."

Moira's insides jolted. Katie couldn't know she already told Father Mark about Mr. Brennan's assaults and her guilt for leaving Katie behind to suffer him. "Why him?"

"Maybe confession will set you free and babies will come."

Moira thought, *I'll never be set free. The sin that stains my soul is not forgivable.* But instead, agreed with Katie. "Yes, I'll try that," and got her off the topic of Father Mark.

Chapter 12
MOIRA MURPHY MCMAHON

BOSTON MASSACHUSETTS

I walked home deep in thought. Katie's advice to confess my sins to Father Mark was on my mind. He's a wonderful, caring priest. He knows I was not pure when I married Paddy, and absolved me. He doesn't know of the sin I cannot bear to speak of. The sin neither he nor even God will absolve me from. I imagined my confession.

Bless me, Father, for I have sinned. I was just to move in with my cousin Mary and fall in love with my future husband. My monthly was two months passed because my employer stole my innocence. Forgive me, Father Mark, forgive me, God. I took his letter opener and cut the child from my womb. I killed my own baby.

———

I planned to live in America since I was a small child. My family in Ireland wasn't destitute like Katie's. We had a small ranch and garden. There was always enough food. I had homespun clothes and schooled to the eighth-grade. If I stayed in Ireland, I would have married a rancher like my da. It wasn't the life for me. My sights were set on America, living in a big city, surrounded by people and shops. The dream of my American life included a husband, home and children. My children would have more than an eighth-grade education, and they'd wear clothes made in a mill and purchased in a shop.

I didn't cry when I left my mam and da. It was me who found work as a nanny for the Brennan's. At almost nineteen, I wanted to start my real life.

The crossing was difficult, but a worthwhile sacrifice for the opportunity to work for a rich American family. The Beacon Street address was in the most affluent neighborhood in Boston. The church was nearby. There were plenty of Irish in Boston. It seemed like a fine plan. It was, until Charles Brennan ruined my life.

I didn't think about the work of a domestic. I could not have imagined it. I'd never seen a carpet or scrubbed floors. We had dirt floors in Ireland. I was accustomed to hard work. On the ranch, we rose at dawn every morning to feed the animals. We birthed cows and sheep at all hours of the night. Growing healthy crops was back breaking.

American life was all new. I didn't know about running water, flush toilets and stoves. The sheer size of the house was daunting with four sets of stairs to climb. The noise from the streets made my head ache. The stiff shoes blistered my feet and my back ached from walking on cobblestones. Worse than all that, Mr. Brennan hated me. He yelled at me every day. I hid china cups that I broke for fear he'd lash me. But I didn't break. I'm strong. I knew I'd adjust. The suffering was worth the chance to live in America.

Mrs. Brennan agreed, with three children to care for, we needed to replace Anne, the nanny who returned to Ireland before I arrived. I saw it as a chance to reunite with my cousin Katie. Why shouldn't she have the same opportunity for a better life as I did? I counted the days of August, awaiting her arrival.

Sleep came easy after each exhausting day. That is, until the night he came into my room. At first, he loomed over me. I thought he came to beat me for being so clumsy around the house. When he climbed on top of me, I kicked and punched. I've tried to block out the moment I realized he was pushing my nightdress up to my waist. Don't know why, but I stopped moving once he thrust himself inside me. There was no escaping the punishment he was bent on giving out.

By the time Katie arrived, I knew my fate. He hated me, and if I wasn't working to his expectations, he'd punish me in the night. I tried harder every day. But he came and went. I buried the secret shame deep inside me. Like poison, it festered and spread to every corner of my being. I withdrew into my fetid self. I thought Katie was safe, she learned faster than me. She cried for home, not because of him.

I felt a surge of happiness when I met Paddy. I tried to be the free and sweet girl I once was, but the nighttime visits caused me to retreat into myself. I wanted to return his love. The poison flowing through my veins held me back. My inner voice reminded me I wasn't pure, I wasn't worthy. I held Paddy at a distance. I feared if he got too close, he'd taste my bitterness.

Imagine my shock when Cousin Mary told me it was common knowledge the English masters bedded their nannies. I already despised myself for hiding my dirty secrets from Paddy, and now the guilt of abandoning Katie overwhelmed me. I should have been content in Ireland. I was cursed for my ambition and selfishness.

Somehow, I moved forward with plans to leave Beacon Street and move in to my Cousin Mary's home. Did I think the guilt and secrets would be left behind? Did I think my two missed monthlies had no meaning? The realization that I was with child washed over me the night before I was to move. All hope of marriage and family was lost. My secret would be revealed. I'd suffer disgrace and rejection.

If Mr. Brennan is evil, what am I for cutting my own child from my womb for the chance to live my dream? My desire for a better life in America is tangled with secrecy, sins and lies. My own body denies me a child every month. I'm rotting from the inside out and driving my loved ones from me.

Dear God, is there a way back for me?

Chapter 13
REVELATIONS

BOSTON MASSACHUSETTS

SPRING 1871…Sturdy purple and green crocuses poked through half-thawed earth. The last of the snow melted into puddles, signaling the end of a frigid, stormy winter and hints of spring.

An occasional penny appeared in the basket at the rear of the church. Paddy and Father Mark's attempts at raising funds for the mission proved futile. Prayers offered by parishioners went unanswered.

The two met in Father Mark's modest quarters. "Paddy, I'm a patient man, but this hard winter robbed me of my energy. I don't think we'll be seeing a mission in Boston any time soon."

"Let's not lose sight of the work we still do, Father. We placed three newborns in good homes this winter."

"We did. Thank you. It's the hundreds we didn't help who weigh on my mind."

Paddy supported Father in his despair. "Don't discount the spiritual care you give the sick and dying. Remember, He spent seven days creating the world. It may take seven years for two of his servants to raise ten thousand dollars."

Father Mark's worn face wrinkled as he chuckled at the remark. He looked up from his spectacles, "You're right, son. I'm an impatient old man. I'll keep praying." He changed the subject, "How's Moira? She hardly speaks to me."

"Father, her heart is broken. She's fixed on conceiving a child and it's not happening. We don't talk about having children anymore. It's too painful."

Father Mark tread carefully, "Paddy, if you can't have children of your own, might you take one of the children we place?"

"That would be a true irony, now wouldn't it?"

The priest grinned and nodded.

"I don't think Moira is ready to consider adoption. It's too soon. And don't forget, I'd be in a spot trying to explain my access to abandoned babies. We'll wait and see."

"Sure, Paddy. Keep it in mind. I've mentioned to Moira I occasionally meet young women looking to give up a child. If it comes to pass, let me be the connection and leave you out of it. In time, son, in good time."

Paddy stood from his chair. "In the meantime, Father, we can't have you feeling discouraged. We need you. The parish depends on your support. It's spring. Maybe the sun will shine on a generous donor and the money will be an Easter gift. Come, let's walk outside."

"Praise be to God. Yes, I need the fresh air."

———

Spring sunshine did not pierce the drawn drapes at 2102 Beacon Street. Katie passed the winter secluding herself there, except for Sunday Mass. She and Moira met at church, speaking briefly each week. Neither shared good news. "I'm still bleeding each month. There's no baby in my future. Paddy married the wrong woman. And look at you. Your skin is as white as winter's snow and you've dark circles under your eyes."

"It's desperate for me, Moira. I spend my days with the children inside the house. When I can, I help Etta with housework. She does the work of two of us. I don't sleep nights, sure he'll appear."

Moira grabbed Katie's hand, "This isn't the land of opportunity for us. I wish we never came to America."

"Aye, I should be home, taking care of my mother and father. They are alone and failing."

"You're no help with no money. You're better off sending your wages so they have food."

The two walked on brick sidewalks still cold from winter frost. "It doesn't feel like spring. The air still holds the chill."

"And the church is bone cold. Let's pray." Moira offered a prayer just loud enough for Katie's ears, "Dear God, please hear us and help us out of this."

Katie made a silent prayer, *and make him stop coming to my room.*

The pre-dawn chats with Rose had continued through the winter. Katie avoided mentioning Mr. Brennan. "We may soon have a nurses' training school right in the parish."

"Grand news, Katie. You'll make a splendid nurse."

"Yes, I think so. At home, as a child, I played nurse. My sister was my patient."

"When will the school open?"

"Oh, not until a miracle happens. Father Mark needs ten thousand dollars. There's an old schoolhouse on the church property, but it needs work. The Sisters of Mercy will come to Boston to run the school when the renovations are finished."

They didn't mention the nighttime assaults. An unspoken understanding existed between the two. Rose reached for Katie's hand, "Katie, dear, this is your opportunity."

"Yes, but without the money, there'll be no nursing school."

"If I could help, I would. As much as I love how you mother my little ones, you need to move on. It's best for you to go, and soon."

Katie let her disappointment show. "It's been the dream that's kept me hoping. I'd train as a nurse and live at the school, away from here. I imagined myself returning to Galway and working in a hospital."

"Don't lose hope, dear. Miracles do happen."

Warm spring sunshine welcomed Easter Sunday. Winter faded, allowing trees to produce the magnificent white blossoms of flowering pear trees. Magnolia blooms dressed the streets with white and purple flowers. Father Mark celebrated Mass, delivering a homily describing the resurrection of hope. He blessed the Easter pilgrims. "Let your spirits bask in the sunlight of hope. Go in peace."

He returned to his quarters and prepared a breakfast of bangers and mash with onion gravy. A courier interrupted his meal, delivering a rosewood box. He examined its unique carvings and jade inserts of flowers and birds. Alone in his parlor, he opened it to reveal ten thousand American dollars placed on the red silk lining. Father Mark looked upward, *Dear Jesus, You have granted us an Easter miracle.*

He sent for Moira and Paddy, leaving the breakfast to grow cold. "Give praise to the Lord. We have our miracle. An anonymous donor sent us the money."

Paddy jumped and clapped his hands declaring he had indeed influenced Councilman Walsh. "It took some time, but, my God, the man came through. He found a wealthy Irish businessman."

Moira thought, *A businessman would want his name attached to such a gift.* Instead, she celebrated the miracle, "Aye, we are blessed for sure."

Father Mark wrote the Sisters of Mercy.

> *My Dear Sisters,*
> *Our Lord provided once again. We will begin renovation and hope to welcome you and our first students next spring.*
> *Blessings,*
> *Father Mark Boyle*

Paddy volunteered to manage the project. He visited Councilman Walsh for recommendations of contractors. "Councilman Walsh, we are deeply grateful for your assistance. We respectfully request your recommendations for reliable builders for this project."

Councilman Walsh, a ruddy faced, rotund man with a head of thick black hair, accepted credit for the miracle. "My pleasure to serve the Irish of Boston. I expect you'll remember this and vote for my re-election."

"For sure, Councilman. The whole parish is behind you."

The Councilman paused. "Paddy, I've taken a liking to you. We need more Irish on the City Council."

Paddy's heart skipped a beat. "You flatter me, Councilman. Now that you mention it, I am interested in Boston politics. I believe we'll see an Irish Catholic mayor in the next decade."

Councilman Walsh blanched, "That's quite a notion, young man. I wouldn't bet money on that just yet. You should attend our Council meetings. You're a fireman as I recall."

"I am, sir."

"We're trying to get approval for a new hook and ladder on Washington Street. It might help our cause if a fireman, an Irish one at that, came to the meetings."

Paddy stared at the black, bushy eyebrow that extended from Councilman Walsh's left to right eye. "Without a doubt, sir, I'll be there."

"Watch for the notices. I'll see you then. And now, let me recommend Sean Landers as a contractor for your project. My own sons and nephews work for his company. He'll appreciate the job."

Paddy left the Councilman's office. He walked at a brisk pace. Thoughts of his future in politics raced through his mind. *Imagine me. Attending City Council meetings. This is my chance. I've already impressed the Councilman. Soon I'll impress more when we open the nursing school.*

Paddy immersed himself in the plans to renovate the schoolhouse. He found Sean an able partner. "Sean, my man, you and I will spend the ten thousand dollars with care. After all, this is God's work, and we can't be mucking it up."

"Aye, I agree. I know of the work of the Sisters of Mercy. Their hospital in Maryland treated soldiers from the South and North with the same care during the war."

Paddy and Sean set to work. Plans for the mission began.

Moira shared the miracle with Katie at Mass. "Our dreams are coming true. Soon, you'll be living in the mission and training to be a nurse."

Katie breathed a sigh of relief, "It's my way out. Let's hope it happens soon. I want my nights of terror to end."

She visited Rose bringing tea and good news. Rose did not ask her to open the drapes to brighten the room. Katie never noticed the missing jewelry box, but even in the darkened room, saw bruises around Rose's eyes. "Oh, dear God, what's happened?"

Rose's left hand covered the side of her face. She did not turn to talk to Katie. "It's no bother, Katie. Come, sit by my bed and tell me about the children."

Distracted by Rose's battered face, Katie probed further. "Am I to blame? Is it because of our talks?"

"Of course, not, Katie. As I told you before, it is very complicated."

Katie dared to speak out of turn. "Mr. Brennan's cruelty takes different forms. I fear we are both victims of it."

"Mr. Brennan's a victim of cruelty himself. He's a hard man to understand."

Aye, I agree with that, Katie thought to herself.

Rose, appearing fragile and small in the bed, continued in her soft voice. "Mr. Brennan suffered hardships as a child. He lived on the streets, abandoned by his mother. When he arrived in America he found work with a furniture maker. He slept on a bed of sawdust and worked for scraps of food. As a young boy, he knew he wanted more out of life." Rose sat straighter in the bed as she told the story. "He spent life alone until he married me."

"How did he become wealthy?"

"Hard work and determination. He spent his youth collecting and studying the discards of others. As years passed, he became a very shrewd businessman, buying and selling fine furniture and antiques."

"Were you ever happy together?"

Rose turned her head toward Katie. She hesitated. "At first, when Charles was born. I thought we were a real family. But soon I realized I had mistaken his greed for ambition and his need to possess me as love."

Katie listened.

"He didn't see me as a wife. My only usefulness to him was to bear children. They were more possessions for him to own. I suppose I was in love with the notion of having a family. We both wanted our first child, Charles. Margaret was conceived when he forced himself on me."

"Why do you stay?"

"More complications, my dear Katie. I have nowhere to go. I'll lose the children all together. I'm afraid my fate would be worse than the isolation of this room."

Katie shared the news of the miracle, but without her initial excitement. She spoke in a low voice, "Father Mark received money for the new mission. What will happen to you if I leave?"

The two women locked eyes. Rose spoke in a motherly tone. "Katie, this is my life, not yours. You must go and find your own way. My place is here, for the children."

There were still unanswered questions. Katie ventured, "Virginia is such a darling child."

Rose stiffened and looked away. Katie continued in a pleading voice. "Charles and Margaret are dear, as well. They have each other, but I fear for Virginia. She is treated differently. You sit and watch the older children at night. You don't go to Virginia's room."

Katie stopped speaking. After a moment of silence, Rose spoke, leaving time between each word. "Katie, Virginia is not my child. Anne, the nanny who left before Moira arrived, gave birth to her in this house. Mr. Brennan is not one to give up his possessions. He sent Anne back to Ireland and kept Virginia."

Chapter 14
CHARLES BRENNAN'S WOMEN

BOSTON MASSACHUSETTS

SPRING 1871... I compare my wife to a fine antique - rare, delicate, lovely to look at, but not to be touched.

The notion of marrying her excited me. I took great care furnishing the marital bedroom. The hand-carved four poster bed and chest were French. The canopy, an exquisite Edwardian Lace. The chest, Phillipe, made of burl wood with bronze finishes. The Victorian chairs, upholstered in light green crushed velvet. Carved bouquets decorate the mahogany wood frames. The legs, cabriole with claw feet. Each piece a discard from the home of a wealthy Boston Brahmin. I envisioned many nights of conjugal bliss there.

I have few sexual experiences. An eighteen-year-old girl in Vermont took my virginity at fourteen. She lured me into the barn, offering a hot plate of food. Before I understood, she had my pants off and her mouth on my cock. Next, she put me on my back and rode me like a horse until I came. Seduction was a game to her. She found my excitement, mixed with fear, intriguing. It ended when her father discovered her riding one of his hired hands.

I paid prostitutes to meet my sexual needs in Boston. It was easier than making the effort to impress a woman enough to have sex with me.

It's simple with streetwalkers. You give them money, they give you sex. Granted, the encounter is usually outdoors in a dark alley. My preference is to be satisfied while laying on Italian linen bedclothes with finely hand-embroidered pastel flowers.

Marriage offered the comfort of a warm bed with a familiar body. Now, I understand the bedroom decorum expected of a proper English wife. The husband's role is to respect her virtue. Engaging in sex is for the sole purpose of having children. My wife shared this view. She also made certain demands on me. At first, I went along with her rules, dutifully bathing prior to conjugal visits. I even brushed my teeth. If I smelled of whiskey, the opportunity was lost.

I often imagined her pure white, silky skin, but never appreciated it with my eyes or hands. She wore a long nightdress which granted me access through a small opening. We never touched each other.

My experience with prostitutes and Rose convinced me women prefer sex to be of a short duration. Rose, like the prostitutes, insisted I finish the act in less than two minutes. I always accommodated.

As a newly married couple, Rose and I shared the canopy bed. She granted me the privilege of intercourse once each month. I took advantage of the full two minutes allowed. We were expecting Charles within the first year. Rose insisted we refrain from marital relations once she was with child. We were both overjoyed when she gave birth. I looked forward to resuming our monthly, albeit brief, relations. She obsessed on the infant.

Charles' birth was another achievement for the London street boy. Regrettably, after he arrived, Rose turned me out of the bedroom altogether. She nursed Charles, refusing to allow me near either of them. I didn't resent Charles. He is my son. Let's just say, he took over the bedroom. Hope of laying with my wife was lost.

When Charles moved to the nursery, I expected to be invited to the marriage bedroom. I missed seeing my reflection in the golden baroque mirror I acquired from a well-known Boston barrister. It had exquisitely carved wood and was decorated with acanthus leaves. No invitation was rendered. Rose needed rest. I accepted this turn, retiring to my separate bedroom. On one occasion, freshly bathed, I visited her in the canopy bed. I expected a warm welcome after over a year of patient abstinence. The reception or lack of, disappointed me. Rose expected me to adhere to the common practice of having sex only to conceive a child and she had no interest in having another child. I, on the other hand, resented having to pay hard earned money to prostitutes for pleasure.

Not one to be discouraged by rejection, I continued to work hard at the business. Trade expanded to every corner of the world. The wealthy were building opulent summer mansions. They wanted expensive, exotic furnishings from China, Italy, India and Persia. I developed relationships with exporters, importers, and freight merchants to secure the most unusual, sought after pieces. Beacon Antiques had a monopoly on imports in Boston. The wealthiest sought me out for advice.

Rose cared for Charles. A convenient arrangement for both, except for the absence of sex. Despite the rules of decorum for marital relations, I viewed sex as my due, in my home. As a child of the streets I learned sometimes you just have to take what you want.

I didn't bathe the night of Margaret's conception. My breath smelled of whiskey. Fair is fair. Rose didn't play by my rules, so I no longer agreed to hers. She looked up from her book when I entered the room. Didn't speak, or even protest. I might have enjoyed that. She just laid there, motionless, emotionless, on my French linens. After that night, she put a lock on the bedroom door.

It became clear my options were limited. Rather than humping a prostitute against a wall in a back alley, I frequented Miss Ellie's Parlor on Endicott Street. Evenings there were most enjoyable. The décor, modest, but comfortable. I often smoked a cigar while sipping cognac. The ladies played a hand or two of cards with me before we retired to a private room. Their perfume and rouge enticed me. The cheap jewelry, attractive, in a strange way. Different from Rose. Miss Ellie's suited my needs for the next several years, although costlier than a quick one on the street, or, of course, with my wife.

William lived with us and cooked the meals. Rose insisted on the addition of a nanny as the children grew older. I hoped the extra help would make her more agreeable. Although I enjoyed evenings at Miss Ellie's, I didn't like paying for a service I should have at home without a charge.

I drew the line at hiring an Irish nanny. The Irish are a stupid lot. What use is a nanny who never held an infant or changed a nappy? They are illiterate, useless as teachers for the children. Half the Irish women in Boston are insane. The asylums are full of them. I didn't want one in my house. Rose ignored me and sent for an Irish girl.

As I predicted, Anne proved an awkward lout. She arrived in rags, half-starved. Rose liked her more than me. She helped her bathe and dressed her in a new frock and shoes. They became friends of sorts. They cared for the children, dressing them up and taking them for walks. I watched them smiling and talking to each other. They shared secrets, I suspect. The distance between us widened. I became an outsider in my own home.

I won't be made a fool. I own Beacon Antiques, the house, my wife, children and the help. I accumulated my possessions by hard work and sacrifice. I began to think of Anne as a possibility. After all, I owned her.

The thought of a mick, Catholic at that, gave me a moment's pause. That passed. The planning excited me as much as the pleasure of the act. I stepped carefully into the dark room. There was just enough moonlight to allow me to see the shock on Anne's face. She was feisty. The fight made my blood run. Her resistance amused me.

In time, she came to accept my affection, which took away some of the enjoyment for me. I'd rather she moved a bit than play dead. Can't say Anne enjoyed the sex, although I tried to pleasure her.

I'd lift her gown and view her body. For the first time, I put my hands on a woman's private parts, exploring every inch of her skin. When I entered her, I lingered. There was no two-minute limit for me.

Typical Irish, Anne whimpered through the whole event. The whining didn't distract me. I controlled the sex, satisfying my every fantasy. I took charge. We followed my rules.

I suppose I should have expected it. Rose found out and had a lock put on Anne's door. It was too late. She was pregnant. The women at Miss Ellie's never get pregnant, or at least, they don't stay pregnant. These stupid Irish don't know how to take care of themselves. Her swollen breasts and thick waist gave it away. Rose took it hard. She stopped speaking to me altogether. She doesn't understand a man has needs.

Rose said nothing when I kept the child. Brennan children are my property. They will not be raised digging potatoes. I named her Virginia and sent Anne back to her beloved homeland.

That's when my wife foolishly threatened to leave me and take my children. I put the fear of God in her for that. It wasn't enough. She sent for another Irish nanny.

Moira arrived. A red-haired harp with freckles. A true peasant. Another one who thought the real English language came out of her mouth when she spoke. Rose dressed and fattened her up. Then, she went to her bedroom and closed the drapes. She hasn't emerged in the daylight again. She knows her place. Of my own doing, I was cursed with another clumsy, mick nanny, and a hermit of a wife.

Moira was useless, as I predicted. As if to make me more miserable, she and Rose sent for another ragged harp to help with the housework and three children. Her cousin, Katie, arrived within a few months.

Moira wasn't a quiet, passive one, like Anne. She was the bouncy, sassy type. A know-it-all harp, always smiling, carrying on about nothing. I changed that fast enough. She was an odd one. Fought me at first and then went limp right in the middle of the whole thing. Most nights I'd find her rolled in a ball as if that could stop me. Another one who pretended she didn't want it. Have to, so they don't appear to enjoy it. After a while she just spread her legs until I finished. I think she understood it's part of the job, pleasing the master. I didn't spend a lot of time exploring Moira. Red heads don't interest me. I had my way with her a few times a week. Her whining put me off. I noticed she stopped chattering around the house. It worked well until she moved out.

That's when I hired a Colored woman. At least they know how to make a bed. Unfortunately, I don't have an appetite for big Negroes. I had only the tall, skinny one left. When she first arrived, she stunk and wore a rag. It was an embarrassment to see her standing on my stoop. Her fingernails still had dirt under them from the fields. She looked better cleaned up. Unlike her cousin, she was quiet and shy. Her youth appealed to me. I wanted to stroke her shiny, black hair. I looked forward to viewing what I imagined were long, shapely legs under her nightdress.

I snuck up on her in the night, too. Never even put up a fight. Just stiffened up and laid still. Strong, though. Had to pry open her legs. Reminded me of Rose, even wore one of her old nightdresses. Katie disappointed me. I expected more of a fight from a seventeen-year-old. I did enjoy her reaction when I put it in her mouth. Eyes nearly popped out. Made me laugh.

All part of a day's work, girl.

I'm enjoying my nighttime trysts, deflowering Irish virgins, one at a time.

Chapter 15
BROTHERHOOD

BOSTON MASSACHUSETTS

SUMMER 1871... News of the miracle spread, giving parishioners renewed hope. God answered Father Mark's prayers. An anonymous donor left ten thousand dollars at his door. The dream became a reality. Soon Boston would offer a school to train nurses.

Paddy raised his glass. "Here's to us, Sean, and the work ahead."

They met daily to sketch plans, determining the cost for construction materials and installing modern heating and plumbing systems. Local men inquired about work. "The Irish have first consideration for jobs."

Sean agreed, "Of course, I put the word out." He reported to Father Mark, "We'll replace the roof first, Father. Have to do the outside work before winter."

The priest raised his hand, "There's one thing. I want you and Paddy to visit the mission in Philadelphia."

"Father, I'm an experienced builder."

There was no arguing. "As the person entrusted with the money, I'm making the," he cleared his throat, "suggestion you visit the good Sisters at their hospital and school. Not a nail will be driven until then." The conversation ended. "I'm tying the purse strings until after your trip."

Paddy and Sean traveled by rail to visit the Sisters of Mercy. The train sped through Connecticut and New York, "You're meeting a remarkable group of women today, Paddy."

"I understand. Father Mark is impressed with their work during the Civil War and since."

"I experienced it firsthand, my friend. These Sisters nursed me back to health during the war. I owe them my life."

Paddy reacted, "Were you fighting?"

"I was among the last to arrive at the Battle of Antietam in Maryland, 1862."

"So you were shot."

The train pulled into the station before he answered. The two men arrived at the hospital to meet Sister Bernadette. Sean, standing six feet, two inches tall, with Paddy, at five feet, three inches, were a mismatched but formidable pair. "There's a feeling here I can't describe. It's like a warm, gentle embrace."

Sean nodded, "Indeed, my man. You're feeling the love of the Sisters and the effects of their abundant grace. You're in a holy place."

A petite woman dressed in white introduced herself. She offered a firm handshake. "Welcome to St. Peter's Hospital of Philadelphia. The Sisters started this hospital before the Civil War. We believe Divine Providence led us here to care for the sick and wounded soldiers."

"Sister Bernadette, I was a patient in your hospital in Maryland for three months. The Sisters and nurses brought me back from the brink of death."

"Bless you, Sean. There is a reason God saved you. You're doing His work now, bringing our mission to Boston. Praise the Lord."

The hospital halls were dimly lit. Daylight from floor-to-ceiling windows reflected on clean floors. The air smelled of a spicy disinfectant. All was quiet except for the moaning of men. Women dressed in white habits and veils moved about in silence, tending to the sick.

Sean asked, "Sister, how many missions do you have?"

"The Sisters run five hospitals, all in the North. We're not welcome in the South. We have one small community of Sisters in Atlanta. They are trying to start a school for Colored children. There's no point to freedom if you can't read and write. Progress is slow with no money or support."

They came to an open ward where twenty men lay wounded or unconscious. Many were missing limbs. "These men will stay here the rest of their lives. The injuries to their bodies or brains are so great there is no hope for recovery."

Sean approached a man in a wheelchair, his legs amputated above the knee. "Soldier, let me salute you. Thank you for your sacrifice." The man stared, but didn't respond.

Sister Bernadette nodded. "He never speaks. Shock from the war."

He fought back tears, "Sister, I had no idea so many wounded were in hospitals this long after the war."

Sister's voice softened, "There are many, Sean. Most are in government hospitals. We do our best to keep them clean and comfortable. Come, I'll show you the school." She led them to a two-story wooden building behind the hospital. "Twenty-four students live here for six months. Three girls share a room. Each has a bed and one drawer in the dresser. Flush toilets are in the hall."

"Sister, how are the students trained?"

"Good question, Paddy. Many girls are poor and uneducated and can't read and write. We have classrooms to teach them. Nurses have to understand the handbook of procedures we've developed for sanitation and wound care."

"And then?"

"We bring them to the hospital to train."

More questions came, "Is there safe housing for women in Philadelphia?"

"Ah, we've learned a lesson or two. Single women in Philadelphia can't afford the cost of housing in good neighborhoods. Most are still sending money home." She continued, "The women board at the hospital. They work hard, through the night, if need be. It's part of their duty to shovel coal into the furnace."

Paddy and Sean studied the foundation and framework of the building. They admired the modern plumbing and noted the size of the classrooms and sleeping quarters.

At the end of the day, Sister Bernadette bid goodbye and blessed the men. "The Sisters are grateful for your help to carry on our work. We will come to Boston when your building is ready."

Rolls of paper filled her arms, "Sean and Paddy, let me share the building plans for this school. You'll need them."

"Sister, thank you for your generosity. Sean and I are most grateful."

"God bless you both."

The men left the hospital and found an Irish Pub to their liking. Settling at the bar, Sean commented, "Father Mark was right. This trip has been enlightening. Let's lift a Guinness to the Sisters of Mercy."

His thirst quenched after the third pint, he slurred, "Paddy, my friend, you are like a brother. Thank you for letting me be part of this project. It was a hard day for me. The sight of those men brought back memories."

Paddy rested an arm on his friend's shoulder, his brogue thicker from the drink, "You are a bit of a mystery, if I do say so. I'm only today learning you fought in the war." His curiosity was made bolder by the Guinness, "You didn't answer my question on the train. Were you shot? Is that why you were in the Sisters' hospital?"

"No, I would have preferred that. My company arrived at the bloodiest battle of the War in time to bury thousands of soldiers." Sean swallowed hard. "That's why I'm a mystery to you. It's a part of my life I try to forget."

Paddy ordered two Guinness.

"I'll never forget the scene. Fields strewn with dead soldiers decaying in the sun, covered in maggots. They'd been there for days. Horses, too. There were bodies floating in the only stream for fresh water. We buried them in mass graves. It was impossible to avoid contact. Half my men fell sick from infection and dysentery. I tried to keep going, but the fever hit me hard. I was in a coma for two weeks." Sean looked at his friend, "I'm grateful for this work so I can finally give back."

"I'm sorry. I didn't mean to make you talk about those days. Let's drink to brotherhood and call it a night. Early ride tomorrow."

The train traveled the reverse route to Boston. The men slept off the effects of the Guinness, waking at the whistle announcing the approach to Boston.

Paddy started the conversation, "There's so much I don't know about you, Sean. You keep to yourself. Is there at least a woman in your life?"

"Now, what woman do you know desperate enough for a lanky old man like myself?"

"I admit, only a rare one might find you lovable, but surely, in all this world?"

Sean howled at the insult. "There's been just one woman in my life."

"Ah, then, a heart does beat in your chest. Now, tell me who she is."

"Was, I'm afraid."

Paddy put his hand on Sean's arm, "Sorry, friend, I shouldn't joke."

"No bother, Paddy."

"Did she die in the war?"

"No. She was a nurse in the hospital. Faith's was the first face I saw when I woke from the coma. She looked like an angel, twinkling brown eyes and glowing skin. Her smile warmed my soul. She fed and bathed me. Taught me to walk again. By the time I was healthy, we were in love."

"Faith sounds like a wonderful woman."

Sean rubbed his hand across his face. His voice cracked, "Yes, she was my one true love."

"And she got away?"

"I asked her to marry me many times. Faith knew better, Paddy. I was willing to accept other people's rejection, and she was, as well. The thought of our future children stopped her. The sons and daughters of a Colored woman and white man would be outcasts in either race. She wouldn't bring children into the world to suffer."

No words came to Paddy.

Sean continued, "Faith was a free Colored woman, born in the North. She was one of hundreds who volunteered in the hospitals for soldiers. Loving her gave me the will to live."

"Faith was right, Sean. She understood the world isn't ready for a white man married to a Colored woman. At least you loved."

"I did, my friend. I haven't since. It's why I work so much. Keeps my mind busy."

"It's been more than six years. Do you think you could love again?"

"Maybe one day, lad. But today, I've got work to do. So now you know more about the secret past of Sean Landers."

"Seems we all have secrets in our pasts too painful to share."

Sean looked at his friend and nodded.

They rode the last miles to Boston in silence.

Chapter 16
A CHANCE FOR LOVE

BOSTON MASSACHUSETTS

SUMMER 1871... Winter and spring passed and Katie occupied herself with the children. She reported their progress to Rose. "I walk Charles and Margaret to school each day. Charles runs ahead and races back to me. Margaret holds my hand and skips. They are full of joy."

"It gives me comfort they have you."

"The children ask for you every day."

"How do you respond?"

"I tell them a nighttime tale of a mother who sits by her children's beds in the darkness and looks over them."

Rose sat propped by three pillows. Katie sat in the green velvet chair, wearing Rose's old nightdress. She continued, "In the story, the mother is caring and gentle and brings them sweet dreams in the night."

"Thank you, Katie. I'm sure it's difficult for them. My heart aches to be with my children. I want to tell stories, play, and sing them to sleep. The day will come."

"Yes, mum."

Rose pulled the bedclothes over herself and laid back, "I'm sure of it. Please, kiss Margaret and Charles for me. Tell them their mother loves them very much."

Katie worked side by side with Etta during the winter and spring. Etta showed her how to keep a proper house. The former slave proved a calming influence on the Brennan household. Unlike Moira, she was an experienced housekeeper and nanny. Katie tried to organize chores and learn the English way of bed-making. Etta taught her to clean, serve, and set tables. The two grew as close as mother and daughter. Etta was a wise woman, past forty and large. Her nurturing extended to the Brennan children. Katie laughed when the children hugged her and disappeared into her bosom.

Sitting on the back porch seeking relief from the heat, Katie read Etta a letter from home.

> *Yer da is failing each day. I do me best to keep him clean and fed. Please send money.*
> *Yer luvin Mam.*

"Miss Katie, you spend your time readin' and writin' them letters. You're nineteen now. Look at you. So tall, with that white skin. Must be plenty boys wantin' a girl with them green eyes and long, black hair."

"I'm not looking to meet a lad. I'll be going to nursing school soon and returning to Ireland."

Etta squinted as if trying to see into Katie's mind. "It ain't natural for a young girl to work seven days a week. For the last six months you only left the house to walk the children to school and for Sunday Mass. And what are you hiding wrapped in that cloak?"

Her concern brought sadness out of Katie. She didn't tell Etta her cloak hid the shame she bore for the acts upon her body. Mr. Brennan's visits were less frequent. A month might pass before he appeared reeking of whiskey. Tears stung her eyes, "Miss Etta, I'm so unhappy. I try, but still can't make a proper bed or remember how to set the table. I'm only good for minding the children. Mr. Brennan hates me. He calls you by name and gives you a day off each week. What am I doing wrong?"

Etta's body filled the rocking chair. Her feet, set on the floor, moved her back and forth. She stared into the garden, shaking her head. "Poor Miss Katie. You ain't doin' nothin' wrong, child. President Lincoln freed the Colored slaves. Gave us rights. Any man touches us, the law steps in."

Katie looked away, *Dear Jesus, she knows what he does to me.*

"These English still own you girls from Ireland, like the white masters owned us. There's no one fightin' for you. Only one way for you, and that's out of here."

Katie repeated her newest daydream, "I'll be going to nursing school soon."

Etta stopped rocking and crossed her large arms over her bosom. "That's good, child. That's good. I had dreams once, too. Was gonna be free. Live in my own house with my family. Raise my boys. See them off to school every day."

"You only go home on Sundays."

"That's right. Still ain't free. Black women get more work than the men. Nobody hiring Colored men around here. The jobs go to the whites. I'm still living in the master's house away from my young ones and husband."

Katie's concern changed from herself to her friend, "Is this a better life than before you were free?"

"I guess. Took three years to get here. Northerners didn't know what to do with us when the War ended. At first we lived in crowded slave refugee camps. They was worse than the plantation. Everyone got sick with cholera and dysentery. Thought the blacks was gonna die there for nothin'. Most went back to the plantations to survive."

"But you didn't?"

"We was the lucky ones. Made our way North. We're alive. Not free."

"Do you still dream of a better life?"

Etta unfolded her arms and rocked back and forth. She stared straight ahead. "Not anymore. Seen too much. Dreams are a way to pass time. Only a fool expects them to come true."

———

Sean and Paddy returned from Philadelphia with renewed enthusiasm. They spent hours each week studying the plans. Observing their evening ritual of a Guinness, Sean confessed, "Paddy, I've a secret. Can I trust you with it?"

Paddy's blue eyes widened, "For sure, brother."

Sean stared at the bar, his voice a whisper. "I've an eye for your wife's cousin."

Paddy set down his glass. "My friend, my brother. Please, not that one, unless, of course, you want to offer up a life of suffering."

Sean laughed, "Aye, my friend, I suffer well. And lower your voice. I told you it was a secret."

Paddy's curls bounced as he shook his head.

"Will an old man of thirty-one interest her? She looks younger."

"Katie isn't interested in a man. Even a tall, fair haired bloke like your-self. She never leaves the house. When we first met, she was an imp, smil-ing and teasing. A looker, too. Long legs, big green eyes. She and Moira always had their heads together, planning and plotting."

"And now?"

"She looks mad. I see her at Mass. She wears that cloak with the hood hiding her head even these hot August days. Keeps to herself. Barely speaks to Moira."

"I see her at Mass, as well. I'm drawn to her. Can't explain it. I don't think she's mad. Maybe sad."

Paddy nodded, "Could be. I know she didn't want to leave Galway. Dreams of going back. Nothing's there. She won't survive. It's her mam and da. They are ill. She has to take care of them. No, she won't bother with the likes of you or any man. Take my word for that."

Sean sat tall, now. Rolling his hand through his blond hair, and smil-ing a boyish grin. "We'll see. I can be charming when I have to."

"And now you're a ladies' man, is it? Are you a betting man? I'll buy the Guinness if she speaks to you."

"You're on, brother. I'll wait for her after Mass."

The following Sunday he made a first effort. "Good day, Miss."

Katie lifted her eyes as she walked from church. She saw a man a head taller with shaggy, blonde hair almost covering his eyes. She dropped her eyes and walked on.

A week later Sean greeted Katie again, "Mornin', Miss."

Katie nodded in reflex.

Seizing the opportunity, he summoned his charm, crooked an eyebrow and inquired in his best brogue, "May I walk with you this marvelous Sunday morning?"

Katie continued, hood over her head, without answering.

Sean changed his tactic the third Sunday. "Miss O'Neil, my name is Sean Landers. I'm renovating the school for nurses."

Katie looked out from her hood. "Pleased to make your acquaintance, Mr. Landers."

He waited, his patience rewarded.

"I'm hoping to attend. Good day, now."

It was the first time he heard her voice. Sean played a game now. "Miss O'Neil, if you're interested, I can tell you more about the school. Shall I walk with you?"

Katie stopped and he caught up with the tall girl covered in a cloak and hood on a hot summer day.

Sean chatted through that first walk. He described the trip to Philadelphia. "Father Mark insisted we go. The Sisters run an impressive school. We are following their plans." Katie didn't speak, staying sheltered by her hood and cloak.

Sean waited the next Sunday. "Miss O'Neil, I thought you might have questions after our talk last week."

They walked together as he answered her one question, "When will the school open?"

Sean gave her more details than she asked for, filling the silence. "I'd say six more months if the winter doesn't slow us. There's room for twenty-four women. You'll be training by early spring."

Katie smiled for the first time. "This is the most excited I've been since my days in Galway."

Sean bowed to the smile. "For you, Miss O'Neil, I will work harder and faster each day."

The weekly walks continued into the fall. Sean made a plan. He cleared his throat, "Miss O'Neil, we've been walking home from Mass for five weeks, now."

Katie retreated into her hood.

"May I have the pleasure of your company at the Saturday social next week?"

Jesus, help me. A voice from the hood spoke, "Yes, Mr. Landers, my pleasure, as well."

Katie and Moira discussed the date that week in the park. It was September. The air was dry and cool. "My mood is so vile. Why does he want to be with me?"

"It was the same way with Paddy. It's hard to open a heart heavy with secrets."

"Aye."

Moira encouraged Katie, "Give him a chance. He's a hard-working man. Paddy says he runs the busiest lumber yard on the harbor. And now he's taking time for the school."

"I don't know. I want to train to be a nurse and go back to Ireland. My da's had a stroke and mam can't care for him."

Moira wasn't listening, "He's tall and good looking in a way."

Rose lent Katie a dress for the social. "You look lovely, dear. Go and have a grand evening with your new friend."

"He's a friend, for sure. I'll pass the time with him until I go home."

"Stop by for tea and tell me about your night."

It was Katie's first outing since Moira's wedding. She smiled at the music and sang along. Sean watched her become more animated through the evening. He teased, "Miss O'Neil, you're a singer, are you?"

Embarrassed but quick, Katie replied, "Aye, have I hurt your ears, now?"

"Not at all. You might find I'll be hurtin' your feet. Shall we dance?"

Katie danced for the first time since twirling in the garden at home.

Saturday socials and Sunday walks became regular events. They walked through the park surrounded by trees with orange and red leaves. Joy filled Katie's heart. "Strolling with you, I'm noticing the autumn colors for the first time." She warmed to Sean's gentle and caring way. "You are so patient with me. I know I go on about missing Ireland and going back."

"I like to listen to you talk. Your eyes light up when you tell stories of home."

"Tell me your stories. Do you have family back home?"

"Ireland is a memory, now. Boston is my home. I came here at twenty. I occupy myself with work. My uncle passed. He was my only family in America."

"Then share your memories."

He smiled, "I'd rather listen to yours."

Katie pressed, "Please."

"I'm afraid they are sad."

"Tell me."

They sat on a bench and Sean took Katie's hand, "I was eight. My mother and sister left Kerry for New York. They were to find my uncle in Boston. He owned the lumber company then."

"Was it during the famine?"

"Yes, 1847. I was too young to travel and stayed back with my grandmother."

"What happened?"

"My mother died of fever coming over. My sister was sixteen. She never made it to Boston."

"Why, Sean?"

"My uncle went to New York. He pieced the story together. She was approached at the dock by a runner. People remembered the young girl working days as a scrubwoman and nights cleaning a bar."

"A runner?"

"Yes, back then, scoundrels approached people as they got off the ships and promised housing and work. They made slaves of them."

Katie waited.

"Are you sure you want to hear this, Katie? It's not pleasant."

"Please."

"According to people living around the docks, she was robbed and murdered one night. She had a few pence in her apron."

Katie leaned into him.

"My uncle searched, but never found her grave. She's buried in a paupers' yard with no marking." As Sean finished the story, tears dropped from his eyes. Katie reached and held him to her.

Chapter 17
FOR LOVE

BOSTON MASSACHUSETTS

FALL 1871...The attraction grew stronger each time they met. Sean and Katie spent evenings and Sundays together, often visiting the construction site. They walked hand in hand. She shared stories of Ireland. "We had little, but I loved the simple life and natural beauty. And I was never lonely, Sean."

He listened with patience, "Aye, I understand. Life in Boston is harsh compared to rural Ireland. Everyone rushes and it's noisy, no doubt. Ireland offers peace and solitude."

"I long for it."

"And the loneliness. Do you feel alone, Katie?"

"I have. Until now." She hesitated. "With you, I'm not alone. It's the happiest I've been in America."

Sean smiled, "You make me happy in America." He stopped. Standing a head taller, he placed his hands on her shoulders. "Will you stay?" He hugged her to him. "I want you with me."

Katie relaxed into his arms. "I want to be with you, as well. You know me better than anyone. I feel safe with you."

"Then it's settled." Sean walked at a faster clip.

Katie slowed his pace. "Mam and da are alone and sick. They need my help."

"We can help them. I'm a resourceful man. Let me find a way. I want a life with you, and a family."

The evening ended and Katie visited Rose. They drank tea and chatted until dawn. "I care so much for him. It doesn't matter he's more than ten years older. I'm mature for nineteen, would you agree?"

"Well, you certainly have matured these past few years, dear. It's what's in your hearts that matters. I watched from my window on Sunday. You make a dashing couple."

"I find him handsome. And kind. Always asking after me." She grew serious, "We have deep feelings for each other. I want to be with him, and at the same time, I want to go home."

"Lots of girls send money home and stay in America."

"Mam needs me. She's frail and da's too much for her. I have to go back as soon as I can work as a nurse in Ireland."

"There's time to decide. It will be a year until the mission is built and you finish school. For now, take extra time for yourself."

"A year. So much can happen."

"You're doing all you can, Katie. Be patient."

Katie returned the tea cups to the kitchen, at the same moment William was opening the door. "William, you startled me. Why were you out this late?"

"Sorry, Miss Katie. It's the only time I go out, in the dark. After all the running and hiding to escape my master…. I'm still afraid, I guess."

"I understand, William. But what do you do?"

"I'll tell you the truth, Miss Katie. You have to keep my secret."

"Of course."

They sat together in the dimly lit kitchen. Katie in her nightdress, shawl around her shoulders. William dressed in black clothes. "I'm studyin', Miss Katie. Learnin' to read and write."

"William, that's wonderful."

"Never had schoolin'. There's lots of us, freed blacks, need to learn. The ones who can, teach us at the African Meeting House. Not sure how the whites would take to us learning. That's why we do it at night."

"You should be very proud of yourself, William. I had schooling in Ireland, but learned even more helping the children with their words and arithmetic."

William sat tall. "My daddy died to give me freedom. He can't see me, but I want to make him proud."

"You already have, William. And I'm sure he's looking down on you from heaven."

"Don't know 'bout that. Not a lot of work for us in Boston, but I'll have a better chance if I can read. Wouldn't want Mr. Brennan to know I'm fixin' to leave some day."

"Your secret is safe, William. I'm fixing to leave, as well. Like you, I want to better myself, be a nurse."

William reassured his friend, "You're a nice lady, Miss Katie."

As weeks passed, Katie entertained Etta with stories of her outings with Sean. Etta helped her slip out at every opportunity. Sean brought her to his lumber company and explained plans to expand. "Today, Landers sells lumber to Boston builders and has its own construction company. I plan to buy land, forests. Soon, we'll be the largest supplier of wood and construction materials in Massachusetts." He added, "And the biggest construction company as well."

"You're an ambitious man, Sean. I wish mam could meet you. My da gave up during the famine. He lost hope and never worked. That made mam's life hard."

"And now it's for you to support them. I understand. I can help."

"Such a generous gesture. I can never ask."

"It's a small price to keep you here."

Katie confided her feelings to Moira on their walk to Sunday Mass, "I'm drawn to him and want to be with him all the time. I've never felt that. He makes me laugh and smile."

Moira's tone was flat. She didn't look at Katie. "Lovely, for you."

"He knows the real me and understands my feelings. I've told him a lot." She glanced at her cousin, "Not about us."

Moira stopped, "Don't. Understand? Do not tell him."

"Of course not."

Moira picked up her pace and ordered, "Marry him. He suits you. Quiet, serious, a working man."

Katie changed the subject, "Sean says the school is opening in early spring. I'll be going home in the fall."

Moira snapped. "Your dreams are childish. There's no life there. I planned to leave Ireland since I was a little girl. America is a country where your husband can find work and earn money to feed the children. It's an escape from British oppression."

Katie's temper flared. "I'm not a child. I'm living up to my responsibilities. Your mam and da are healthy and living well. You're not being fair."

They were close to church, and Moira sobbed, "Oh, Katie. I'm sorry. You're right, I'm not being fair. I'm so sad."

She offered her usual reassurances. Moira would have none of it, "I had a dream, too. And it's ruined. I don't even get pregnant. My monthly comes and goes. Paddy doesn't mention children. He's never home. More concerned with the City Council meetings or helping Father Mark repair the church ceiling."

"Let's go to Mass and pray, Moira. Ask Him for help."

Moira thought to herself, *It's God who's punishing me for making myself miscarry with a letter opener. I'm not expectin' help from Him.*

Moira pulled Katie close, "Please, don't leave me. What will I do?"

"A baby will come. In time. Life will be happy even without me."

Months passed and November brought bitter cold, freezing the ground. Hard packed snow stood twelve inches high. Katie pressed Sean, "Will the school still open on schedule?"

"We'll do what we can during the winter. Can't work in a blizzard."

Katie's desperation showed. "You don't understand how important this is. I have to start school soon."

"For sure, but, think, it's more time for us to be together." He tried to warm her.

She resisted his embrace. "You don't understand. No, Sean. Please."

"Have you considered my proposal?"

114

"You proposed?"

Sean laughed, "No, my love, not marriage, as you might be thinking. My only proposal to date is to send money to your mam. I'm hoping the other proposal will follow and be positively received."

Distracted by the offer, Katie replied, "Of course. I'm grateful, Sean. Mam's alone now. I have to think. I don't have an answer right now."

By Christmas, the frigid, snowy winter brought construction to a halt.

Katie and Sean attended midnight Mass. She wrapped her cloak and hood around her body, insulating herself from freezing winds. They walked home bracing against the cold. Sean chatted along the way, pointing out festive candles in every window. Katie listened without comment. When they reached the house, he uncurled a cold hand revealing a gold heart-shaped locket. "One side has my initials. I want *K. O.* on the other side."

She stood shivering on the icy walk, staring at Sean's outstretched hand. "Sean, I want to say 'yes.' I can't." She didn't look at him, but beyond him. "Not now. Not ever."

He snapped his hand shut and replaced the piece in his pocket. "You're a mystery, Katie O'Neil. Have it your way. I've done all I can to win you over."

Katie climbed the stairs as Sean walked away. Neither looked back. She knocked on Rose's bedroom door. "Come in."

She collapsed to her knees and leaned her head onto Rose's lap. "What's wrong, dear?" Rose smelled of fresh linen and a light, crisp cologne.

Katie sobbed, "Oh, I'm lost. I'm seven months with child. What am I to do?"

Rose stroked her black hair, just as she comforted Anne. "I'm sorry. I've been praying this wouldn't happen. I should have taken this into my own hands."

Katie lifted her head and looked at Rose. Tears streaked her face, "And have him beat you to death?"

"I'm not sure I could have stopped him. How long have you known?"

"Haven't bled since June. I've hidden my growing for months. But I can't deny the stirring inside."

"Of all of us, only Moira escaped his abuse."

The tears stopped, she lifted her head and looked at Rose, "Moira escaped him?"

"Yes. I asked her several times."

"And she said he didn't come to her at night?"

"Yes." She assured me.

Rose took Katie's hands. "How can I help?"

"Rose, Moira lied. He raped her until the day she left this house."

Shock covered Rose's face. "Why didn't she tell me?"

Katie shook her head, "Shame. Moira can't bear to admit it happened. She would never tell you."

Still on her knees, possibilities for the future washed over her. Hysterical, she clutched the bedclothes. "Will he put me on the street if he finds out? Will he take my baby? I can't support a child. I can't go home with a child. What will happen to me and my baby?"

Rose stood from her bed, now. She lifted Katie to her feet. "Here, come sit."

Katie climbed into the four-poster mahogany bed and looked at the lace canopy from the inside. The luxurious coverlet and linens warmed her trembling body. "Sean wants me to stay in America. He'll take care of my parents. I wanted to agree, now..."

Rose clasped her hand. "Sean will understand."

Her answer was firm, "No, he cannot know."

"He's a good man, Katie."

"Yes, he is. Why would I burden such a good man?"

"He may understand and accept you and the child."

"I'm afraid he would. And find himself married to a disgraced woman. I can't ask so much of him."

Rose comforted her, "Tell me what you want."

Katie calmed. She thought for a long moment. "My only choice is to go home. I was foolish to think of staying."

"And how will you support a baby and mam?"

"I'll finish nursing school." She added with conviction, "My baby will not be raised in this house."

"You're too upset to make important decisions. Perhaps your child can live in an orphanage until you finish school. There are religious orders who take in children. Let me contact them."

Katie listened as thoughts raced through her mind. *Sean can never know. Rose will help me...I must hide this...*

Rose's voice interrupted her thoughts. "Mr. Brennan cannot learn of the baby. I'll lose control if he finds out."

"He won't. He never looks at me." Katie looked at Rose, "It's been three months since he visited me. I hope he's lost his manhood to the rich food and whiskey."

Rose nodded with understanding.

Katie left to the sound of Rose's words, "Rest tonight, dear. I'll take care of this."

Chapter 18
ROSE ASHFORD BRENNAN

BOSTON MASSACHUSETTS

Mother and father raised me as a proper English woman. Mother was demure and gentle. She expected to be treated as a lady and deferred to by her husband. I modeled myself after her.

When my father died, I was on my own in America and found myself needing to work in a shop to supplement my small inheritance. It wasn't my plan to marry, but with circumstances as they were, I found it necessary. Charles was not the ideal candidate for a husband. He was gruff even when he tried to be charming. His grammar skills, an embarrassment. His personal hygiene habits, poor. In many ways, our marriage was an arrangement. It met both of our needs. He wanted a proper wife to enhance his image as a businessman. I wanted security. I loved him in a pitying sort of way. He suffered a difficult childhood and persevered, becoming successful despite his limited intellect. He didn't press me when I insisted our marital relations occur only at the time of the month when we were likely to conceive a child. It's the way of a proper English woman.

Neither of us were experienced in the bed. No words of love or endearment were exchanged. Each encounter repulsed me more. Charles was clumsy and brutish. He laid on top of me, crushing me with his weight. I endured his grunting and wheezing in my ears and held my breath for fear of smelling his. It was as if he was mating with a cow. I tolerated it for seven months before conceiving Charles.

The fragile strings holding us together as husband and wife frayed after my son's birth. I devoted myself to him. Charles spent his time making money. It was not my intent to have another child. Margaret's father was raving mad drunk the night he forced himself on me. It's a wonder the child is so lovely given the circumstances of her conception. He stopped visiting my room after that. The stench of cheap perfume convinced me he was satisfying himself at the local brothel. The years passed. I cared for the children, he immersed himself in Beacon Antiques. It seemed the arrangement worked for us both.

William cooked and a scrubwoman cleaned once a week. As the children grew, our needs changed. I wanted a nanny to take them to the park and help with their studies. Charles was reluctant, but acquiesced. Anne, our first nanny, and I became friends. She was a young, innocent girl, fresh from Ireland. I enjoyed the company of another woman in the house. It was less than a year after she arrived I learned she was carrying my husband's child. There was no discussion with me. He kept the baby girl and shipped Anne back to Ireland. I can't recall feeling such rage. I defied him and sent for Moira.

It's not my nature to be confrontational, but after learning he abused Anne, I threatened him. He seemed to find humor in my anger. He threw back his head, exposing inflamed gums and rotted teeth. The notion of me, a scorned wife, leaving him and taking the children, amused him. When he stopped laughing, anger occupied his face. I didn't see it coming, but I heard the thud and in an instant realized he'd punched me in the cheek. The protruding knuckles of his fat fist broke the skin on my face. He hit me again in the stomach. I fell to the floor and he kicked me in the kidney. He was screaming, but I couldn't hear his words.

I endured a flurry of kicks from his booted foot. I crawled across the floor to escape his rage and huddled in a corner. He stopped and put his scarlet face close to mine. His glassy eyes bulged as he pulled my hair and bent my head back. He spoke, saliva spraying my face, his breath toxic.

"After you greet your newest little harpie, you'll stay in your bedroom. No one threatens Charles Brennan. You are my possession, as are the children. Threaten me again or leave your bedroom, and I'll divorce you. I'll say you are a whore and see you begging in the streets. You are a woman.

You have no rights to my property or my children. Remember Rose, it's the bedroom for you or the streets."

I nursed my wounds and cared for the children until Moira arrived. Her spirit impressed me, even if her domestic skills were inferior. My husband's cold stares warned me to retreat to my room. If I was with the children, he'd walk up behind me and pinch and twist the skin on my back. My last act of defiance was to send for Moira's cousin. With me locked away, it would take two to care for my children and tend to the housework.

I passed the days alone in my darkened room. Sweet Moira brought meals and tea. She'd tell me of the children's activities and progress with their studies. At night, I'd tiptoe to Charles' and Margaret's room and watch them sleep.

On several occasions, in the subtlest way, I asked Moira how she and Mr. Brennan got on. Each time she assured me, if anything, he ignored her. I was at peace knowing she was safe. Perhaps my threat had some effect.

Katie was different. She changed after Moira moved out. At first, I thought she was missing her cousin. The words were never spoken between us, but I knew. The innocence was gone from her face. He was brutalizing her. I was helpless. I prayed she'd move on before becoming pregnant, like Anne. It's too late. She's with child.

I tried my best. I couldn't stand up to him and risk being put to the streets and losing my children altogether. I stole ten thousand dollars from the cash box he hides in his library. He pummeled me about the face when he discovered it missing. I'm scarred from the cuts his prized Georgian diamond cluster ring left below my left eye. I convinced him I gave it to charity. This time I came closer to being put out. He warned, "I'll let this go with just a beating. Defy me again, Rose, and you'll be spreading your legs for sailors on the docks and thanking them for scraps of food. Mark my words."

I offered the beating as penance for my cowardice. I believed he'd put me out if I stood up to him. Sending the money for the nursing school was all I could do to save Katie. It was that or kill him.

Chapter 19
LIVES MERGE

BOSTON MASSACHSETTS

JANUARY 1872… Katie helped Etta prepare Christmas dinner. Her cloak hid a swollen belly from people at church, but Etta knew a pregnant woman's body. "Child, don't do no heavy work now. I'll be doing the liftin' for a while."

She looked at Etta. Her dark eyes were warm and understanding.

Christmas night Katie slept after an exhausting day. She stirred at the odor of whiskey. A dark figure stood over her. *I thought he was done with me. God save my baby.*

In a drunken slur, he uttered, "Merry Christmas to me," mounted her, satisfied himself and left.

The next day Mr. Brennan summoned her to his library. Standing in front of a roaring fire, he dressed in his usual dark suit. He spoke, never lifting his eyes. "Miss O'Neil, I understand you are with child. You are a disgrace. Because I am a compassionate man, you may stay in my home until the birth. When is it due?"

Katie stared at the carpet, "In two months, sir. February."

"I assume returning to Ireland is preferable to a life on the streets." He uncrossed his hands, pointing toward his desk. There lay a ticket for steerage passage for one adult. "I'll take the fare from your wages."

"There's only one ticket."

"Correct. There's no future in Ireland. The child will stay here."

Katie cried to Rose, "He's taking my baby and sending me back."

"Katie, don't despair. I'll do what I can. We have time to think of a plan."

Katie stayed in the house after Christmas eve. A cloak no longer hid the growing life inside. Her Beacon Street family, Rose, Etta and William helped her through long days.

She sat in the kitchen, stacking plates. "Just stay put, child. We can take care of the cleaning."

"I can help, Etta, really."

"You're doing fine. Back in the days I had my boys, weren't no one helpin' me. I was bigger than you. Birthin' them near killed me."

Katie's eyes widened. Her fear showed. "Killed you?"

Etta retreated. "Not killed me, like dead. Just hurt a lot. Don't worry, Etta will be there. I'll take care of you."

"You got me, too. Me and Etta. We gonna be right by your side. Every day. Right, Etta?"

"William's right. Let us do the worryin'. You rest much as you can. Spend time with the children. Read them books."

"I can walk them to school."

"No need. Too icy for you. Mrs. Brennan agrees. Let me do it."

Katie spent hours sitting in bed with Rose. "It's best to keep your feet up. They'll fill with water."

"I'm useless. Look at me. The maid sitting in bed with the master's wife. I should be serving you."

"Not to worry. It's my husband who caused this. I'm responsible. Besides, I enjoy your company."

Katie smiled. "Thank you, Rose. I don't know what I'd do if you didn't care so much. Has Mr. Brennan mentioned me? Did he change his mind about keeping my baby?"

"He doesn't speak to me." Rose changed the subject. "Have you heard from Moira?"

"If I see her, it's at Sunday Mass. I've stopped going since Christmas."

Rose hesitated, "Sean?"

"He sent two notes. I didn't respond. He's given up."

Sean hadn't given up. He sat over a Guinness with Paddy. "Katie O'Neil is a mystery, my friend."

"She's a strange one. I told you. What did she do now?"

"Disappeared on me." He snapped his fingers, "Gone. It took weeks before she allowed me to walk with her. We grew close after a while. I thought we were in love."

Paddy took a swig of Guinness. He shook his head, "Sorry for you. But you can't say I didn't warn you."

"I offered to send money to her mam. I hinted about marriage. At first, she seemed open. Then, on Christmas eve, she ran faster than a scared rabbit."

"Seen her since?"

"No sign of her at Mass. I sent two notes to the house. She hasn't answered."

"Did she go back to Ireland? Something she'd do. Moira would know."

"Can you ask her?"

"I will, but don't expect an answer. We don't talk much these days."

Moira was sullen and lost in a world of guilt. *There's no hope for a child. I'm sure God struck me barren for my sin.* She was lonely. The distance between her and Paddy was growing. Paddy spent days at the firehouse and nights absorbed in City Council meetings.

They ate dinner in near silence. Paddy used caution introducing the topic of Katie. "Have you seen your cousin at church lately?"

"Can't say I have. You spend more time there than I do. Have you?"

Paddy moved toward his wife. "Moira, I'm at church for a good reason. Father Mark needs my help."

"Your wife needs you, too. You work all day and are off at Council meetings or church every night."

"Sorry, dear. Perhaps I'd stay home if you were more agreeable."

Moira didn't respond. "I'll call on Katie if I have a chance."

"Thank you. Sean is concerned. She's not answering his notes."

Moira changed her tone, "Paddy, I'm sorry. My mood is so foul. We should be looking after Katie. I'll see if she's well."

Paddy kissed her on the forehead and brought her to him. "I love you, Moira." The sign of affection from her husband brought tears to Moira's eyes. They held each other in silence.

Moira sent a note addressed to Katie O'Neil at 2102 Beacon Street. A week passed with no response. Not to be ignored, she walked to the house from church on Sunday. She climbed the back stairs to Katie's quarters.

Moira found Katie sitting on a rocker loaned by Rose. Her face swollen, and body great with child. The sight shocked her. She made the sign of the cross, "Dear Jesus, Mary and Joseph."

Katie sobbed, "Please, don't be telling anyone. He's sending me back to Ireland and keeping the baby. Same as he did to Anne."

"Virginia is Anne's child?"

"Rose told me. He made Anne pregnant and sent her off."

Katie's sobs grew louder. "Last night I dreamed I took my last breath of air in this evil house."

"Katie, no."

"I was in my grave, buried by the crush of people on the streets. I could still hear hooves on the cobblestones, and turning, grinding wheels of carriages. My tombstone stood atop my grave. It was this house, etched with the words, *Here lies Katie O'Neil in America.*"

Moira knelt to comfort her. "What can I do? Can I tell Father Mark?"

"No, please. Just let it be. I can't fight."

"Yes, you can. You're strong. Stronger than me. Don't give up. We can get help. Maybe Mrs. Brennan."

Katie laid on the bed. "Aye, Rose has a plan. We'll try to hide the birth from Mr. Brennan and send it to an orphanage. Etta and William are helping."

"An orphanage? Why? It's your child."

"What will I do with it, living on the streets? That's where I'll be once it's born."

Moira paced, "No, never. You have us. There's another way."

Katie curled up and wept. "I hoped to finish school and have the baby back. I'd go home then. But, he's putting me out. He's bought my ticket."

Moira's concerns for herself disappeared as she comforted her cousin. "Let me tell Paddy. Sean, does he know?"

Katie's great belly made moving an effort. She tried to sit up. "No, please Moira. There's a reason I didn't tell you. I don't want them involved. I have to save my baby from a life with Mr. Brennan. Promise me."

Moira sat on the bed, "I promise. I won't interfere with your plan."

Katie covered her face, crying out to Moira, "Why, why is this happening to me?" She placed one hand on her belly, "How can I love this child so much but wish its father dead?"

Moira urged her cousin, "Calm yourself. It's not good for you or the baby. Please, try to rest." Katie laid down. Moira stayed, stroking her back until she fell asleep.

Hours later Katie awoke to a dark room. Her bedclothes were wet. Pains came every ten minutes. She woke Etta. "The baby's coming early. It's time." Etta birthed many babies. She began preparations and summoned Mrs. Brennan.

"She's in labor, come now. Mr. Brennan is asleep in his chair after drinking his whiskey."

Etta dressed Katie in a clean nightgown. She prepared chamomile tea to help with labor pains, and boiled water. A pile of clean white rags sat by the bed. Rose comforted Katie who endured the pains without calling out. She gave William a note. "Go to this address. The driver will come and wait ten houses south of the house." The plan was in motion. Once the baby arrived, it would be transported to an orphanage west of Boston.

By midnight Katie labored hard. She begged for Moira. "Please. I need my dearest friend."

"I'll go, Miss Katie." William seldom ventured out. And now, ran through the streets for the second time in one night. Frigid air stung his lungs making it hard to breathe. He reached Moira's home and banged hard on the door. Moira sat in the kitchen, waiting for Paddy. She never slept until he returned. This night he was repairing the ceiling of the church. She startled at the knock and the face of a black man at the door. Recognizing William, she got her cloak. They ran together to Beacon Street.

Breathless and freezing, Moira crept up the back stairs to Katie's room. She took in the scene. She found Rose dressed in a nightgown and bed jacket, hair loose. "Come in, Moira. Katie's been waiting for you." Etta sang in a low, rhythmic voice to take Katie's mind off the pain. Moira moved to Katie's shoulder with Rose on the other side. They wiped her brow and stroked her head.

The women kept silent for fear of waking Mr. Brennan. Katie muffled cries into a blanket. After two hours of labor, she cried out to push. Etta ran for the boiling water in the downstairs kitchen. "Good Jesus," she hollered as her brown eyes popped wide at the sight of Mr. Brennan.

She returned with the water and news. She whispered to Rose, "It's Mr. Brennan. He's in the kitchen." The baby would not be whisked off tonight. Rose and Moira lifted Katie from the shoulders and with one final cry, she pushed out the baby.

Etta received the baby. Joy of the miracle drained from her black face as she viewed a tiny, motionless infant girl. The room fell silent as Katie, Rose and Moira absorbed the tragedy. The baby was dead.

Etta wrapped the tiny body in rags to show Mr. Brennan. He looked and left the kitchen mumbling. "The idiot girl can't even birth a live baby."

Katie laid back in exhaustion. Not able to cry, she closed her eyes.

Rose spoke first, "Moira, please. The driver is waiting ten houses away. Can you go? Dismiss him."

"Of course." Moira donned her cloak, covering her head. She took time to walk and breathe the cold night air. After counting ten houses she spotted the carriage parked in the shadows between gaslights. Without lifting her head, "You may leave, sir. There is no package to deliver tonight."

"Moira?"

Peeking from her hood she looked inside the dark carriage. "Paddy?"

"What are you doing?"

"What are you doing?" She recovered. "Go home, Paddy. I'll explain later. You will as well."

Moira rushed back to find the quiet of Katie's room replaced with frantic activity. Katie was sitting up, calling out, "Ohhhhh, Ohhhh, I need to push. What is it?"

Rose checked to find a black-haired head crowning. She looked at Katie, then Moira. "There's another baby."

Moira held Katie while she pushed. Rose coaxed the baby's head out. With another push, the body emerged. Rose held a fully formed, lifeless baby boy. She turned her attention to the afterbirth. "Moira, please take him. Wrap his body."

Moira held the boy, feeling his warm, moist skin in her hands. She noticed clear fluid coming from the baby's mouth. Out of instinct, she removed it with her finger and placed her mouth to his. She breathed four gentle breaths. *One for each of my lost babies.* On the fourth breath, the baby's color turned from white to pink as he gasped for air. He made tiny sounds at first, then wailed until he glowed bright red. The mood changed to elation. The room filled with laughter, tears, and hugs. Moira brought the baby to Katie who kissed his head. She then took the infant to the furthest corner of the room. "We don't want Mr. Brennan to hear his cries."

Etta assured, "Don't worry about him. He's dead drunk."

Rose turned to Moira, "We dismissed the driver. We have to take him away from this house tonight."

"Father Mark will help. He'll find a nursing mother in the parish to keep him for the night. We'll have the driver bring him to the orphanage tomorrow."

Katie, exhausted and weak, fought sleep. She mumbled, "No, no orphanage for my son." Revived, she looked at Moira. "Take him."

Moira cradled the infant to her breast. "What, what are you saying?"

"Take him. Give him a chance. He deserves a family. Raise him, love him. I can't."

Rose agreed. "Go, now, Moira, before Mr. Brennan discovers us. Give him a good life." Rose made a silent vow. *My husband will never hurt anyone again.*

Moira didn't think. She ran down the back stairs into the cold January night. Clutching the swaddled infant, she wrapped her cloak around him. She reached Father Mark's residence, knocking with one hand. He opened the door to find her breathless and wild eyed. Her hair strewn around her shoulders and face, she was holding an infant.

"Father, it's Katie's son. Just born. She sent me off with him so Mr. Brennan doesn't take him."

"Come in, child. You're freezing."

Moira rushed through the story, "Only you know what Mr. Brennan did to us. This is his baby."

"Calm down, Moira."

"I will, Father. He's sending her back to Ireland and keeping the child. She had twins. The girl, born dead. I ran off with this child before he found out."

"We have to find a wet nurse to feed him. Let me take him to Eileen Foley. Stay here."

Once Father returned, Moira finished the story. "Katie can't raise him. At first, he was to go to an orphanage until she finished school. She can't care for him, Father. She wants me and Paddy to adopt him."

Father shook his head and mumbled, "The unselfish love of a mother."

In the excitement, Moira forgot about Paddy, "Father, Mrs. Brennan hired a driver to bring the baby to the orphanage. When the girl was stillborn, I dismissed him." The priest, still wearing his winter coat over his robe, lit his pipe. "Why do you suppose my Paddy was the driver? And I thought he was repairing the church ceiling."

He exhaled. "Ask your husband. The child is safe and fed. It's for you to convince Paddy to come to church on Sunday and adopt this child."

Chapter 20
A FAMILY

BOSTON MASSACHUSETTS

JANUARY 1872... Moira walked home through freezing cold streets. The events of the evening occupied her mind. *So many secrets. So much deceit. And now, a son. Is this a message from God? Am I forgiven?*

She thought about her husband. *Paddy? Have our secrets and lies driven us too far apart? Can we rekindle our love? Tonight he'll learn the truth from me. What are his secrets? The carriage. Why is he driving babies to an orphanage? It's time for honesty. No matter the cost.*

She arrived home to find him sitting at the kitchen table. "Holy Mary, Mother of God, where have you been? You look a fright. Why are you out in your house clothes?"

Her temper flared, "I could ask you the same, Mr. McMahon. Where have you been?" Moira's red waves fell loose around her shoulders. Her cloak opened, exposing blood soaked clothing. She looked at herself and then at her tired husband. "Paddy, luv, I have so much to tell you. Please, listen."

Moira sank into a chair. Reaching across the table, she held his hand. "I'll start at the beginning. I came from Ireland expecting to find Anne at the Brennan home. We were to tend to two children and housework. When I arrived, she was gone. She left an infant behind."

Paddy stared at his wife. His hand went limp in her grasp as his anger left him. "Her own child?"

"Yes. I learned of this tonight. Mr. Brennan made her pregnant and kept the child." She spoke in a slow, soft voice. "I was on my own. I didn't know how to keep house. Mr. Brennan screamed at me for breaking his china."

"I remember you telling me."

"Mrs. Brennan stayed in her room. I thought the infant was her baby. I was left to do all the work. The only other help was William, the cook. I convinced Mrs. Brennan to send for Katie. I'm to blame for what's happened."

"This story is hard to follow. What's happened? Why are you covered with blood?"

Moira cried. "You may not love me or stay with me when I'm finished, but I can't live with myself anymore."

He stood and moved toward his wife. She rose from her chair as he reached to hold her. "Moira, there's nothing you can say to make me stop loving you."

"Before Katie arrived from Ireland…oh, this is hard."

"Tell me."

"Mr. Brennan had his way with me."

Moira sobbed. Paddy held her closer, clenching his fists. He swallowed hard. "You did nothing wrong. I'm so sorry. I wish I'd saved you from it."

"There's more."

He moved away. Looking at her now, his arms on her shoulders, "What more can there be?"

Weak and exhausted, she collapsed to the floor. "You and God will never forgive me."

Paddy sank to the floor. "Luv, what is it? What is tearing you apart?"

There, embraced in her husband's arms, Moira confessed her sin for the first time. "It happened the night before my move to cousin Mary's, the start of our courtship. My monthly, I missed it twice…I, I couldn't have his baby…or lose you…or face the shame."

Paddy touched her hair. His voice cracked, "My Moira, you've suffered so much."

"I ruined myself. I'm sure of it. There'll be no children for us. How can you or God forgive me?"

"You don't need my forgiveness. As for God, the God I know loves you. Ask Him and He'll forgive." He paused and rocked her in his arms, "I need you to forgive me. I've stayed away from you. Couldn't bear your sadness. I'm sorry. I should have been with you instead of off every night. I've been blind and selfish, lost in my own ambitions."

They cried together, for Moira's pain, the lost babies, Paddy's sadness.

"Paddy, there's so much more to tell."

"It's seven in the morning. I can't imagine."

He helped her to a chair, "Go on."

"I thought the night visits from Mr. Brennan were his way of punishing me for being a poor housekeeper. I tried to learn the American way. I was wrong. When I moved out, he turned to Katie to satisfy himself."

"Why didn't you leave sooner?"

"And go where? The tenements are filthy with disease. I had no one to tell. I was ashamed. I suffered alone."

Paddy nodded with understanding.

"He got her pregnant, too. He's sending her back to Ireland after the birth. I helped tonight. Katie gave birth to a stillborn. That's what Mr. Brennan thinks."

"Thinks?"

"Yes, she had twins. A boy and a girl. The boy is healthy. He's with a wet nurse now. Father Mark brought him there for me."

"For you? Father Mark? How did he get involved?"

"I brought the baby to him. I had no other choice." Remember, I sent you away?"

"Moira. One stillborn, a live baby. Did you take the baby and run away? What are you trying to tell me?"

"No. Well, yes. We hid him from Mr. Brennan. Katie gave us the baby."

"Have you lost your mind?"

Moira reached for Paddy's hand, "I have not. Listen. Be patient. Katie is going back to Ireland. Mr. Brennan is sending her. It's what she wants. She can't raise a baby."

Paddy was up pacing and running his hands through his mop of curls, "I don't know. Who else is in on this scheme?"

Moira rose, "Scheme? We're trying to save a child from a life in a love-less home."

Paddy persisted "Who else?"

Moira changed her tactic, "Mrs. Brennan, for one. She arranged for the carriage in the first place."

Paddy responded. "Father got the note to send the driver. We just knew where to wait. Didn't know who sent for the carriage. Go on."

"Katie is involved too, of course. At first she planned to take the child to Ireland after nursing school. Tonight she realized he needed a good home here in America...with us."

They were standing face to face. Paddy folded his arms over his chest, "Do you understand what you're saying?"

"I do. We all agreed. It's what's best."

"All? There are more people involved?"

Moira dropped her eyes and whispered, "Etta and William. The other maid and the cook."

"Moira."

She looked at her husband, "Please, Paddy. You weren't there."

Fatigue overcame Paddy, "We need to think more. We can't make a decision about a child tonight. There's so much you don't know."

Moira's voice grew stronger, "Yes. About the carriage. What is the secret behind it?"

"What did Father Mark tell you?"

"He told me to ask you. What's going on? Why were you driving the carriage?"

Color drained from his face.

Moira turned somber, "There's nothing you can say to change my love."

Paddy dropped his eyes. "I've never touched Irish soil. Boston is my birthplace."

"Go on."

"Father Mark was a young priest when he found a baby at his door."

Moira waited.

He stared at her.

Her voice, tender, "Where did you grow up?"

"Father took me to an orphanage run by Irish Sisters in Lowell. They were caring and kind. Some of the boys were adopted."

"And you?"

"No, not me. People were poor. They adopted the strongest boys who could work and help the family."

Moira coaxed more from Paddy. "How did you come to Boston? Who are your mother and father?"

"Father Mark visited the orphans whenever he brought a new baby. He became known in Boston to women who had to give up their children. I looked forward to his visits."

"Go on."

"Is this hard for you to hear?"

"I'm sad, Paddy. You had so little as a child."

"Not at all. The Sisters were tender and loving, and Father Mark, a father to me. But I ran away."

"From the orphanage?"

"Yes. To find my mother in Boston. I wanted to live with Father Mark while I searched for her. I was sent back each time. I left for good on my sixteenth birthday."

"And Father took you in?"

"Yes."

"I'm confused. You told me you were from County Clare. And, your brogue."

"Aye, you assumed and I let you. The Sisters and Father influenced the brogue." He paused, "You see, I carry shame, too. I feared you wouldn't marry the son of a streetwalker."

"You found her?"

"No. It's likely she was an Irish girl turned prostitute."

Moira tightened her grasp of Paddy's hand, "I love you. Your past doesn't matter."

"We're exhausted. Let's sleep. We can talk more after we rest."

They laid together, eyes closed. Paddy's heart pulsed hard. Fury swept through him as he thought about Mr. Brennan. He reached for his wife's hand and whispered, "There will be justice for you and Katie." His mind shifted, "A child. Is this right for us?"

Moira opened her eyes and rose from bed. "I'll make tea. There'll be no rest until we sort this out."

They drank tea and talked more. "You still haven't explained why you were driving the carriage last night."

"I lived with Father Mark for two years. I watched him take in abandoned babies. They were destined for a life on the streets, but for the kindness of others. I help Father find good homes for them. If need be, I drive them to the orphanage."

"Father Mark is a good man."

"He saved me, and now, together, we save other children. We keep our work secret to protect the women."

"I would have understood."

"And I, you."

"Our love for each other is strong."

"It is. This child, perhaps it's God's will for us to give him a chance at life."

"Aye, we already have. He was lifeless when I first held him. God was with me when I breathed life into him."

"What do we do?"

"He's with a wet nurse for now. After Sunday Mass, Father Mark will present the baby for adoption. We'll step forward."

"I can't answer now. My head aches after hearing what the monster did to you girls. I won't be at peace until he pays."

She pressed for a decision. "Sunday is in two days. We can't let this baby go."

He thought of Mr. Brennan, *I'll be introducing you to Satan.* "Let's try to sleep. I have to think."

Moira laid awake, *Please, God. Move Paddy to welcome this child.*

Sunday came. Paddy and Moira sat in the first row of the church. After Mass, Father addressed the parishioners. "Good morning, my brethren. Today I offer two infant boys for adoption into your homes."

Moira gasped, "Two boys!!!! Which is ours?"

The infants laid side by side on blankets. One wore a white linen baptismal cap embroidered with an Irish cross. Paddy and Moira stepped in front of him.

Paddy whispered a prayer. "Praise be to God for this gift, a child born of the suffering of others. We will keep him safe."

Etta helped a frail Katie to a seat in the last row in time to see Father pass the baby. "He's in their hands, Etta. Let's go home." Sean watched from the shadows as they left the church.

The new parents stood outside while friends congratulated them. Moira glowed, "This is our son. Thanks be to God."

As they walked home, Paddy, cradling baby Neil in one arm, Moira asked, "How do you suppose the baptismal cap made it to the baby?"

Paddy's wide grin spread from ear to ear. "Aye, I learned another boy was left at Father's door. I found the magic hanky Katie gave you on our wedding day. Mrs. Foley stitched it to a cap for our son."

"Thank you, Paddy."

He put his free arm around her and pulled her close, "There's been enough calamity in this family."

Chapter 21
PADDY MCMAHON

BOSTON MASSACHUSETTS

Moira and I walked home from church. Our son, Neil, in my arms. I stood tall, smiled, held my wife's hand, but I wasn't proud of myself. The turmoil of the week occupied my mind. So many secrets and lies were finally untangled. My heart ached knowing my wife, a sweet, innocent girl, was raped in the dark by a monster. The pain and shame nearly crushed her, and I, her husband turned away, leaving her to suffer alone.

I thought about my own motives and actions. Perhaps I created distance to keep her from knowing my secrets. I'm the son of a prostitute. I don't know who my mother was and I'm sure she didn't know the man who fathered me. Did I think being a hero, a fireman, a politician, a rescuer of abandoned children would erase the circumstances of my birth? Why didn't I rescue my own wife?

Father Mark is a true hero. He labors quietly and seeks no glory. I live because of him. My mother left me in the snow, wrapped in rags. Father Mark was returning to his quarters after giving the last rights to a dying man. As he tells it, the night was freezing cold, snow on the ground. He sensed movement and looked to his right. I was there, just hours old.

I wasn't the first child he'd found. Father left a candle burning in the window as a beacon for lost mothers. If not for that flame, I'd have been abandoned in a dark alley, left to freeze to death.

The good Sisters in Lowell were my family. Not everyone there was an orphan. Some were left by destitute parents no longer able to feed their children. Few of us were adopted. People were too poor to take in other children. Occasionally a farmer would adopt an older boy as a hand. I was small, no one wanted me.

Father Mark was the only man I knew as a child. I'd wait for him to arrive at the orphanage with an infant. He always had a piece of candy or bread for me. I'd practice my fiddle and play for him. He'd smile and clap to my tunes. I pretended to myself that he was my father. One time, when I was ten, I stowed away in his carriage. He gave me a cup of tea and a bowl of soup and brought me right back. I ran off several times after that. Not that the Sisters weren't good. I wanted to find my mother. I was sure she was looking for me in Boston.

I turned sixteen and Father Mark took me in. He had no choice, I showed up at his home, unannounced, for the second time. It wasn't long before an infant was laid at his door. He brought it in from the cold, tiny, alone, helpless. I saw myself, a shivering baby, wrapped in rags, abandoned on a priest's doorstep. The loneliness of my life overwhelmed me. I knew my mother wasn't searching for me. No one was.

Father enlisted me to bring babies to the women in the parish who'd agreed to nurse them until they were brought to the orphanage. It was humbling work. When I went off on my own, I continued to help. Becoming a fireman was a proud moment for me. Once again, I was humbled to do God's work.

Somewhere I lost that humility. Ambition took me over. I created my own identity. I was Paddy McMahon, with a slight Irish brogue and a wry grin. A dandy fiddler, Boston firefighter, and aspiring politician. I turned my back on my wife and poured my energy into making a name for myself. I busied myself with the nursing school, City Council meetings, and helping Father Mark. Noble work for a blind husband.

The events of this week have restored my vision. My wife and son are my family. At last, a family. The work I do for others and the City of

Boston will be to enhance their lives, to protect women from monsters, to assure the children of immigrants have an education.

I got lost for a while. Paddy McMahon is a good man. He'll be a giving husband and his child will have the love of a caring father.

Chapter 22
CHARLES BRENNAN IS NO FOOL

BOSTON MASSACHUSETTS

MARCH, 1872…I recognize a pregnant woman when I lay on one. Discovered it when I visited her. First time in months. Lost interest for a while. Whiskey gives me more satisfaction than two minutes of thankless sex with a long-legged pot licker. There's no pleasure in love-making when she just lays there, legs stiff, holding her breath until it's over. English, Irish. The same. Why don't they lay back and enjoy it?

The deceit incensed me. Who does she think she is? Living under my roof, eating my food, carrying my child. Did she expect I'd never notice?

Set her straight the next day. An unmarried pregnant maid is a disgrace to this home. I told her. She's off to Ireland after the birth. The child stays here. No child of mine will grow up barefoot in a mud hut.

My instincts told me to be aware. Rose concocted a plan to deceive me. I'm sure of it. The girl slips into her room and they gossip until sunrise. They think I'm in a whiskey stupor, but I hear the whispers. I wasn't surprised they plotted against me. Rose delights in acting contrary to my wishes. It's what brings her pleasure these days. She's destined for the streets.

Sure enough. I was right. It was a bitter cold night late in January. Something was happening. I knew when William avoided me at dinner.

He's my only company. I settled in my library for the evening. Went soft on the whiskey to stay alert. The first of the scuttling began close to midnight. Bided my time and checked the kitchen. Water boiling on the stove confirmed it. The girl was in labor. Etta shuffled into the kitchen faster than usual. Went white when she saw me. Eyes near jumped right out her head.

I understand Rose being in on the ruse. She hates me. Etta, she's only a slave woman. What should I expect? But William? After letting him work for me all these years? Giving him a place to sleep in the kitchen. That's disappointing. I imagine they planned to sneak the baby and girl out of the house and back to Ireland. A fool's errand for sure.

I waited in the kitchen. They were caught. My plan was back in place. The child stays here. The girl goes to Ireland. Before long, Etta brought me good news. A stillborn. Saw it myself. I make girls. It's my third one. Might have cared if it was a boy. Stupid mick couldn't even push out a live baby. I celebrated with some whiskey and retired to my bedroom. One problem solved. Now I just had to get the girl out of my house. I slept well.

Control of the household shifted after that night. Rose, a different Rose, came out of her room. She took charge of the house. Her voice, strong. She even looked taller than I remembered. I decided to let it go until I got the girl out of the house.

I planned to put her on a boat back to Ireland a week after the birth. It's easy to recover from a stillborn. No baby to care for. She stayed three months. Rose's doing, of course. Out of my hands. Something about losing too much blood. I watched her and the girl come and go from the house. Talking, making plans. Rose doesn't speak to me. Her defiance is securing her fate.

The business keeps me busy. Beacon Antiques is growing. I spend less time collecting old furniture to concentrate on global trading. My collection of mercury glass doorknobs is fetching a pretty penny. French birdcages are the rage. The wealthy fashion them as lanterns. Not my taste, but imported and sold dozens of them. My hand-painted drawings from India are in vogue. I'm expecting a shipment of fine Japanese porcelain and hand-blown Venetian glass this month.

I was successful, making money. A reward for Charles Brennan seemed due. Now, I'm a sexual man. Rewards of the flesh please me. Can't help myself. Etta came into my mind. I've never been with a Negro. The notion of lying on a big black woman with large bosoms intrigued me. I'm used to small-breasted, bony whites.

This feat took careful planning. Rose might be anywhere these days. The Irish one roams the house at all hours. I stayed sober Monday and waited in my library until after midnight. Intending to surprise, I took off my boots. In my stocking feet, I tiptoed to Etta's room. Her door was unlocked. I crept up to her bed, already aroused. She was deep in sleep. Her snores, loud as thunder. Stepping closer to the bed, dropped my pants.

I pounced. Poor Etta. Her mouth and eyes popped. I moved fast, lifting her gown. I inserted myself and felt the pleasure. She tried to howl. I muffled her voice with my hand. The fight delighted me. More fun than the sex. She flailed her arms, punching my chest. I held them down. She kicked me. I thrust myself into her and pressed my weight on her legs. She smashed her forehead against mine. Stars floated in front of me. She cursed me to burn in hell. The pain of her punches and kicks, mixed with the euphoria of penetrating her, excited, no, exhilarated me. I finished in spite of her protests. It was glorious. Best sex I've had. I won't be wasting my time on stiff-legged white girls. I'll be back for more Etta.

The next day the spring sun brightened my mood. I thought Rose was leaving me when I saw her Italian leather valise by the front door. Even better, it was the girl. I'll let the valise pass in favor of a smooth exit. It's another sign of Rose's rebellion against me. I'll tend to her later. For now, I look forward to morning when the livery takes Miss Katie O'Neil to the port. Later, Etta and I will celebrate with a spirited tryst.

I'll spend this evening in my library in the company of a glass of whiskey. Dear Etta, must have liked it as much as I did. She refreshed my antique Victorian glass decanter with my finest scotch whiskey.

Chapter 23
BEGINNINGS AND ENDINGS

BOSTON MASSACHUSETTS

SPRING 1872... Rose Brennan emerged from her exile. "Etta, I'll read to the children and put them to bed. You've done enough today."

Etta nursed a weak, frail Katie back to health with love and food, "Here, honey. I made chicken soup with biscuits. This will help you grow stronger."

"Thank you. You are so good to me."

The older woman shook her head, "Such a young girl. Crying shame, what he done to you. An innocent. My people take care of their own. Whites send you away."

Katie's physical strength returned over the weeks. Her ghost white skin turned a healthy pink and Etta's cooking brought weight back to her body. Her sadness lingered.

Rose visited each day. "Forgive me for being a burden. Etta is doing all the work. I'm sorry for not helping."

"Katie, please, rest. Etta is fine. I enjoy time with the children. I've missed them. What can I do for you? You're so melancholy."

Tears flowed, "I'm so empty."

"I can only imagine. You've lost Sean and your babies."

"I can't be with Sean. I'm a disgrace. My babies, I carried them for months, loved them, tried to protect them. And now, one's dead, and I can't see my boy."

"Let me arrange for a carriage and a visit with the baby. Only you can decide about Sean."

Katie cried into her hands and nodded.

Moira's guilt and shame lifted after absolution from Father Mark. Motherhood restored her confidence. She welcomed Katie's visit. "Hold your son. We've been waiting."

Weak from the ride, Katie sat in the rocker. Her face opened with joy. "I pictured this for so long. Pink cheeks, heart-shaped lips." Pressing her nose to his neck, "I imagined the scent of new life."

"You gave us a wonderful gift. We can never repay you. Neil brings so much love into our world."

"It's you and Paddy who gave me the gift. My son will grow up with a loving family and home. You saved him from a life on Beacon Street, unloved."

Rose stood nearby. Tears pooled in her eyes. "Katie, I'm sorry I haven't been a good mother. I promise to be in their lives now. No child in my home will be unloved."

Weeks turned to months. The Brennan home changed with Rose as the mistress and mother. She and Etta worked together. The house filled with sounds of laughter and child's play. "Etta, have you noticed? Mr. Brennan spends more time locked in his library now that the children are playing in the house and garden."

"And he been drinkin' more, too. I fill his empty crystal bottle with whiskey every night."

Katie's body healed with time. It was a day in late March when she walked to Moira's house. The two bonded closer by their love for Neil, "You are a loving mother, Moira. Much like my own mam."

"I hold him and think how much I love him. And then I remember how much we've suffered."

Katie responded, "Aye, I have the same thoughts. I'm living in the house with the monster who brought so much pain to our lives. And with a short walk, I hold his son who's captured our hearts."

Moira never disclosed her sin to Katie. "You're brave, cousin. I never...I couldn't have done the same. And here, he's brought us so much love and happiness."

Katie smiled at Neil.

"Will you be happy, ever, Katie? I want that for you."

Moira didn't wait for an answer. She put Neil in his cradle and prepared tea.

"Do you hear of Sean? I confess, he's on my mind these days."

"I don't, except Paddy says he's working long days to finish the school. The first class is early summer. June, I think." Moira waited. "I could deliver a message through Paddy."

"No, no. Thank you." Katie breathed in. "Look what I've lost. A daughter, a son. A man who loved me. I came here a naïve girl, full of spirit. I'm leaving, a broken woman. Moira, my only hope is the memories fade when I'm home."

The two sat together, holding hands. Moira reminded, "Out of the pain, we have child. We'll always share him."

"Aye. What will you tell him about his birth?"

"Paddy and I talked about this. When Neil is old enough to ask, we'll tell him the story of his birthday. He'll learn about the three ladies who greeted him with gifts. His Aunt Rose brought him angel wings and set him free. I was there to breathe his first breaths with him. And Aunt Katie O'Neil, who shared her green eyes and black hair and most of all, the gift of life itself."

"It is a wonderful birth story. Moira, I'm at peace. This was meant to be."

Katie walked home at dusk. The late March winds sent a chill through her. She didn't wear a hood, but allowed the cold to wash over her face and hair. *I wonder if Sean thinks of me. No, no. I wonder what Sean thinks of me.*

Word from home prompted the decision to leave. "I've received a letter. Mam's failed since da died. She can't be alone. It's time, Rose, for me to go home."

The carriage was due before dawn. Moira woke Neil and prepared him for the farewell visit on Beacon Street. Paddy arrived home in time to join them. "You've had a long night. Another mission of mercy?"

"Aye, you could say that. I'm a tired man today."

Rose and Etta waited with Katie in the downstairs kitchen.

"Where's William?"

"In a mood. Keepin' busy cleaning pots."

Rose dressed in a deep green taffeta jacket with braided white silk trim and matching skirt. Her hair not in its usual long braid, but a stylish French twist. Moira, Paddy and Neil arrived. Moira commented, "You look lovely today, Mrs. Brennan."

"Thank you. Today is an important day." She glanced toward Katie, "one of endings and new beginnings."

Moira turned to her cousin, "You don't have to go. You can live with us."

"Thank you. Mam is waiting. I have to go to her."

Katie held three-month-old Neil. She stared into his green eyes. Her tears fell on his soft skin. Moira whispered, "Kiss your boy. We love you so much. I promise he will make you proud."

An exhausted Paddy swallowed the lump in his throat. His voice cracked, "You are always welcome. You are part of our family." He started to add, "And Katie, no harm will come to you…" Moira broke in.

"Enough, Paddy."

William peeked from the doorway, eyes shiny with tears. Katie smiled back at him. Rose wrapped an arm around Katie's waist, pulling her close. "Be safe, my love. I will always be here for you. I'm 'Aunt Rose' to Neil. We are all family."

"I pray no harm will come to you for helping me."

"No need for prayers, dear. Trust I will be well."

Katie's head throbbed and chest ached as she pressed the baby to her breast. In halting sobs, she assured her son, "Always remember I carry you in my heart." And to her American family, "God bless you. It's His will I return to Galway. My beloved home."

Etta stood in the darkest corner of the kitchen lost in thoughts of her own. *He ain't no man. He's a pig. No man lays on Etta Jones unless she says so. You come up against the wrong woman last night, Mr. Brennan. The wrong woman.*

Rose moved toward Etta. Her smooth white skin and sloped nose a stark contrast to Etta's round black eyes and flat nose. She took her thick, brown hand. "It's up to us to run this house and care for the children."

"Yes, Missus. It's you and me now. C'mon, Miss Katie, I'll help you with your bag."

The driver stowed the neatly packed valise. Dressed in a new cloak and linen and cotton dress, she boarded the carriage. Another passenger greeted her. "Katie, good day. Will you allow me to ride with you?"

"Sean."

"It's so good to see your face. I'm sorry for what you've been through. You've sacrificed so much."

"Sean, I've missed you. My life is full of turmoil and grief. I carry so much shame. I can't expect you to forgive me."

He moved to her. "The shame is not yours. If I had known, you never would have carried this alone."

The carriage moved along the streets toward the harbor. "Katie, you're a courageous woman. I love you more knowing you are so strong. You deserve better than banishment to Ireland."

"It's my choice. Mam is failing. My sister in England has two young ones and can't help."

"Then let me help. How will you survive?"

"Rose saw to it. She's been very generous. I'll be fine for a while."

"And then?"

"Oh, Sean, I'm not sure these wounds will ever heal."

"I've been wounded, too. It takes time. If it helps, you have me, loving you and waiting."

Katie reached for his hand, "Is this love, what we have?"

"Yes. I closed my heart to love many years ago. It's only to you I've opened it again. I won't lose you."

"I'm too damaged. I want to be worthy of your love."

Tears welled in his eyes. He held her chin in his hand, "Then I'll let you go because I love you. Take time to mend. Lay on the fresh green grass and feel the healing warmth of the Galway sun." He offered a book, "It's a collection of my favorite poems. Think of me when you read them."

She reached and held him for a long embrace. "I do love you. I just can't be here right now."

He kissed her cheek. "When you gaze at the moon over Galway Bay I'll be looking at the same moon here in Boston. And remember, I'm waiting for you to come back to me."

Katie boarded the ship to Liverpool. The mate greeted her, "Good day, ma'am," and directed her to the first-class deck. She found her cabin, closed the door and wept for the Irish waif who ventured to America four years before.

Moira and Paddy walked home with Neil in his pram. "Paddy, you're squeezing my hand too tight."

"Sorry, my luv. Lost in thoughts about my night."

They placed their son in his cradle, making the sign of the cross, thanking God for this gift. Moira touched the white cap with the Irish cross hanging over the cradle.

Rose crept into Virginia's room just before sunrise. She picked up the sleeping four-year-old. Inhaling her sweet scent, she rocked and sang the lullaby she wrote for her other children.

Your mother is here, now. I hold you tonight, my child, so blessed.
With mother's arms around you, I pray this night you will rest.

William's screams pierced the peaceful silence. The windows rattled throughout the house. "Miss Brennan, Miss Brennan, come quick."

Rose sat for a few more minutes singing Virginia back to sleep.

You are surrounded by my love, as angels watch you from above.

She walked out of the nursery and down the stairs toward the screams. She held her head erect and smoothed her green taffeta skirt.

The cries came from the library where Etta cradled a distraught William. He wailed, "Miss Brennan, Lord save us." William held one hand over his mouth. His running nose and tears made wet tracks on his black face. He extended his other hand, pointing to the floor. An ashen Charles Brennan, dressed in his custom tailored black suit, lay dead, sprawled on a rare Persian carpet. A Waterford Crystal Lismore glass, half full of fine scotch whiskey, at his blue finger tips.

William cried, "Miss Brennan, I came for his whiskey bottle. I wash it every morning."

Rose looked at him and then Etta, "Call for a doctor to pronounce him dead." And to William, "Go now, have a cup of tea, calm yourself."

William wiped his face with his apron, "Yes, ma'am."

Rose lifted her skirt and stepped over her husband. She walked toward the windows, *Let's let sunshine and fresh air in this house.*

Chapter 24
KATIE O'NEIL

GALWAY IRELAND

SPRING, 1872...Images swirled in my mind as I sat in the cabin listening to the grind of the engines tasked with crossing the Atlantic. I shed enough tears to fill the ocean that stretched between me and my dream of going home. I conjured memories of the young girl dancing on the breezes in the green fields of Galway. Had evil swept the girl away forever? She dreamed of saving her family, but couldn't save herself. I grieved my babies. My dear daughter. Did she whither in my womb for want of my love? I longed to hold the son I'll never mother. And Sean, sweet and caring. A chance for love, lost. My heart ached. The journey of the girl who traveled to America in a muslin dress was ending. She returned home, a woman bearing shame and guilt.

I thanked God when my feet touched Irish soil. My heart leapt as the carriage approached the cottage. Once again, I was sixteen, innocent and happy. I strained to see mam in the garden, arms outstretched welcoming me to her breasts. She'd hold me until memories of the past disappeared. I'd be home again. Safe.

Mam wasn't in the garden. I found her, shrunken and frail, in the wooden chair. "Mam, I'm here for you now. I've missed you so much."

"Who is it?"

"It's me, Katie. Your girl."

She lifted her head and opened her eyes. Gnarled fingers touched my face. She attempted a smile.

I spent the next weeks nurturing my mother, brushing her hair and bathing her. I removed the tangle of rags wrapped around her body. I heated water in the hearth and gently washed her dried skin. She slept in my clean, white nightgowns. Hot tea and soup nourished her. I cleaned the cottage, wanting to restore it to the days before I left for America. When she woke from sleep, I reminded her of our days as a family. "Do you remember the garden? The herbs we grew? The rabbit stews you made for me, Eileen and da?"

She had but one memory, and repeated it every day. "Da? Have you seen him?"

At times, a glint of recognition appeared in her eyes. I reminded her, "Mam, it's me Katie. Your girl." She raised her thin arm and touched my face each time. After two months, rest came. The deep lines on her face faded with the peace. The young woman who dreamed of a family is in paupers' field reunited with my da again.

I thought about my family after mam passed. Mam and da were matched by neighbors. Married at seventeen, they lived in a two-room cottage on rented land. Da grew a fair crop of potatoes their first two years. When the famine came, he had no crops to sell. My sister Eileen and I were born after those years. Mam kept chickens, and we lived on the money she got for the eggs.

When the potatoes grew again in Ireland, the land we lived on didn't produce. Da's crop was only good enough for livestock feed and us, of course. My father drank to ease the sting of failure.

Da loved us. When he got drunk, he'd cry and tell us so. Mam made us a family bonded by love and faith. She used flour sacks to sew our dresses. They were bleached and softened in the sun. We sang songs as she brushed and braided our long, black hair. Each night we thanked the good Lord for our blessings. And when the time came, she loved us enough to let us go for a life better than hers.

The warm summer days drew me out. I walked through the meadowlands and along the river to Galway Bay. I sat for hours watching the blue water sparkle in the sun. It was more magnificent than I remembered.

My new eyes saw the cottage as cramped, dark and damp. Smoke from the hearth drifted through a hole in the thatched roof. Rain soaked the thatch and kept the dirt floor damp. Water gathered and formed puddles that never drained. The only light, or hope of fresh air came through the one door. I let summer air flow through the cottage and made a bed of dry, fresh straw each night. Crickets chirped an evening lullaby as I drifted to sleep. Bird songs woke me each morning. I knelt in the garden using my hands to move soil and plant seeds for flowers and herbs. My heart warmed at the signs of new life springing from the earth. I began to feel renewed.

I looked forward to letters from Boston. Rose and Moira described walking the children in the park. Neil smiled and giggled now. I wondered how many more children Father Mark has found at his door.

And when I wanted my heart to sing, I envisioned Sean, with his boyish face and blonde hair obscuring his eyes. I locked my eyes on the moon knowing his eyes were on it, too. I read the book of poems he gave me. At first the words had no meaning for me, but in time, as my heart softened, I understood. *Once the heart has known love, it never forgets.* I prayed Sean hadn't forgotten.

Each quiet day brought more peace and healing. The nightmares stopped and sad memories faded. Other memories of America returned. I remembered my friends, Etta and William. The kinship with Moira, and Rose, my treasured confidant. My days filled with reading, remembering, and tending my garden. I walked to the village to post letters and buy food. It was my only contact with others.

One cool day in early fall I noticed a figure in the distance. The morning mist hanging from the sky covered the face. My heart leapt as the tall man with golden hair emerged. Sean's kind face smiled at me. I ran down the road and into his arms, "Is it you? Are you a vision?" My pulse raced. "How did you come here?"

"My sweet lassie, I am real. I came from America, on a ship, to see you."

"I, I, I,"

"I know, you're just so happy to see me."

I clapped and jumped like a child. "That I am, I am."

"Good, then I'll have another hug."

We passed hours talking. "Katie, if only you told me. I can't imagine how lonely you were."

"Aye, I look back and don't understand. How can a man be so cruel? Did he have a conscience? Why didn't I fight back?"

"It's hard to imagine what drives another person. He was a selfish, hateful man. He's gone now. The devil has him. There's no need to fear him."

"Gone? Mr. Brennan?"

"You didn't know? Yes. Dead on the floor the day you left."

My mind wandered back to that morning. I remembered listening from my room to hushed voices. I wondered why doors were opening and closing so early in the morning. Sean's voice brought me back. "You were very young and afraid. It's a fate too many Irish women suffer in silence."

He reminded me of the evil that led to his sister's death.

"So you understand how hopeless I felt. I held on with the thought I could become a nurse and make a better life for myself."

"For me, the nursing school gave hope to other women, like my sister and you. That's why I worked so hard for it."

We walked and talked each day from dawn until darkness. We shared the beauty of Galway, the open, endless sky, the smell of the salt air, the mountains, and wildlife. We held each other at night, realizing our love under the stars.

Sean had more news. "The school opened and received its first students. Rose Brennan and Etta are raising the children and expanding Beacon Antiques."

"I'm so happy for them."

"They spend little time with antiques these days. They're importing Italian marble, carpets from India and expensive French Provincial furnishings."

"Sounds as if they are managing well."

"They are more than managing. Rose employed Etta's husband, Nathan. He receives and delivers the goods. Etta goes home every night to her family."

"How wonderful for her. And you, Sean?"

"There's a building boom in Boston. I purchased acres of forests in Maine and New Hampshire. I'm providing the lumber. I'll be busy for the next three years, and richer for it."

I waited to hear news of Neil. "He's flourishing. I make funny faces and he roars laughing." Sean twisted his face, "See?"

"Please, don't do that. Your face will stay that way."

"You'll see when we get back to Boston."

We, I thought. "We?" I said aloud.

"Yes, we. I won't let you go again, Katie."

I swept my arms across the fields of wildflowers, "But Ireland."

"Darling, Ireland is in our hearts and souls. We don't leave her behind. We take her with us."

Sean wrapped his arms around me and whispered, "Come with me. Be my wife."

I said final prayers at mam and da's grave and took the crucifix hanging over the hearth. Sean and I returned to America.

My husband was right. I didn't leave Ireland. She's still part of my very being.

The End

Made in the USA
Lexington, KY
16 March 2018